Battery is running low

By Moxie

Förlag: BoD – Books on Demand, Stockholm, Sverige

Tryck: BoD – Books on Demand, Norderstedt, Tyskland

ISBN: 978-91-7699-795-6

To: The queers, the mentally ill.

It gets better, you're doing great.

Chapter 1

Sharpener

I look at my phone, the time says one nineteen AM. I've been trying to sleep for three hours, but I really don't feel tired. I look up at my ceiling, the room is spinning, the walls are melting. I begin thinking. The kind of thinking that hurts me more than I realise. I'm talentless, ugly, and fat. I don't deserve anything. I say things like that back and forth in my head for at least twenty minutes. I cry, silently. I take deep breaths to calm down. It doesn't work.

There's only one thing left to try.

I turn on the light on my bedside table before taking out a pencil sharpener blade from the drawer. I pull up my sleeve and make five cuts on my wrist. I roll over and fall asleep. Maybe someday, I could fall asleep without harming my body first.

*

Hi, I'm Alyssa Tucker. I'm sixteen years old, and I'm a useless human being. I'm honestly just waiting to die. I pray that it happens soon. A lot of people would describe it as depression, suicidal thoughts. Might be, I don't know. I've been having somewhat "dark thoughts" ever since my dad died last year in a fire. Some sick idiot decided to burn down his office. My dad tried to escape, but it was too late.

I took a few days off from school, and then I stopped going to my singing lessons. I was never much of a singer anyway. It's fine, really.

Ever since dad's death, I've been going to therapy. We all have. Me, mom and my little sister Annie. While mom and Annie actually talked about their feelings, I've been refusing to open up. I don't go to therapy anymore. Annie goes occasionally, and mom goes every week.

It's been hard for all of us. Mom is kind of angry at me for refusing to open up. "Your therapist is only trying to help you" she says. I don't need anyone's help. I can get through this on my own. With my sharpeners and my journals.

I wake up to my stupid alarm, seven AM sharp. I feel like I've only slept one single second. I am drained. I lay in my bed scrolling on social media for a few minutes, before I get up and look in the mirror. I look disgusting. I really need a shower; my hair is greasy and I smell bad. I don't have time to take a quick shower though, let alone wash my hair. So, I think of the next best thing - dry shampoo and deodorant. I still don't smell the best, so I spray on some of the perfume that dad got me for my birthday last year. I curl my eyelashes and put on a ton of mascara. It's really clumpy, but I doubt anyone will notice. After all, I am just a wallflower. When I look and smell OK, I go down to the kitchen for breakfast. Mom is stressed as usual.

"There you are, Ally", she says, as soon as I walk into the kitchen.

"Morning, mom."

"Eat your breakfast quickly. We must leave in fifteen."

I make myself a sandwich and sit down next to my little sister, Annie.

"Could you help me with my maths homework?" she asks.

"I'm sorry, Annie. I have to get ready", I say, eating as fast as I can.

She looks disappointed. I don't blame her. Mom has always been stressed out about something since dad died, so she can't help either one of us with anything. It hasn't exactly been doing much for my grades.

When I've finished the sandwich, I quickly run to the bathroom and brush my teeth. When I come out mom and Annie are already standing in the hallway, waiting for me.

"Come on, you're going to be late", mom says as I'm tying my shoelaces.

"It's fine", I say, throwing my coat on. "Let's go".

We drive to school, and during the ride mom is interrogating us to make sure we brought everything we need for the day. She drops us off at the school gate, and I run inside so I won't be late. I see Eliza Goldberg, my best friend since preschool, standing by my locker. She notices me and smiles.

"Ally!"

"Elz!"

"How are we doing today, love?" she asks me.

"Alright." I open my locker and take off my coat.

"You smell really good."

"Thank you", I say, not entirely sure that she really means it.

Even going back as far as we do, I'm not sure why we're still friends, to be honest. Eliza's got a lot of friends that are way cooler than me. She's an only child with rich parents, and is both pretty and talented. The very opposite of me.

Eliza is tall and has long, curly, light blue hair, beautiful fair skin and gorgeous blue eyes. She's been taking dance classes and piano lessons for as long as I've known her, and she's really good. I don't think that I'm good at anything, actually. The singing lessons didn't work out for me. I'm convinced that I am talentless. I'm short and have boring, straight, brown hair. I have lots of acne, and even my eyes are different from Eliza's, dark brown with a kind of gloomy gaze. I want to be Eliza so badly. I want to be pretty, rich and talented. Not this ugly, poor dork. It's unfair.

We go to class, and it's really boring. The more I listen to Miss Smith, our English teacher, the less I understand what she's saying. I can't take it. I plug in my earphones and turn my music on. I close my eyes, and there it is… my happy place. When I open my eyes again, a piece of paper lies in front of me. It's an assignment, hooray… This day could not get any worse, and it's just starting. I silently start working on the assignment. I don't have a lot of time to work, but I still try to get a few things done.

"Alright class", Miss Smith suddenly says. "We don't have much time left, so you are all free to leave."

I gather my things and start to get up from the chair.

"Oh and Alyssa, could you stay, please?" Miss Smith quickly adds.

Just my luck, I think to myself. After everyone has left, Miss Smith closes the door and walks towards my desk.

"Alyssa, I've noticed that you've been struggling lately."

Struggling? How did she know? Did she see the scars, or did she hear me cry in the bathroom? Or is it about dad's death? I quickly have to think of something to say.

"Oh no, I'm fine."

"I mean, your school results have been dropping."

"I know", I say, looking at my feet.

"I have a suggestion, Alyssa. Would you care to listen?"

"I guess."

"A new student will be joining us tomorrow. His name is Theodore. He's a rather gifted kid."

"What does that have to do with me and my grades?" I ask, slightly annoyed.

"I want you to welcome him to the school", Miss Smith continues. "And before you say no - I think it could be good for you to socialise with other people your age. You could actually learn a lot from him."

"I have friends. I have Eliza", I reply.

"You can have more than one friend. Please give this a shot."

Obviously I refuse, but she keeps pushing it. I finally agree. I really don't want to meet new people, especially not some gifted kid who's supposed to help me study. I'm not that bad at schoolwork.

Instantly afterwards, I have to tell Eliza. So during lunch I approach her while she's talking to a few of her other friends.

"Hey Elz!"

"Oh, hey Ally, What's up?"

Her friends give me disgusted looks. I kind of hesitate for a second, considering telling her another time. Her friends start whispering about something and they finally walk away without saying a word.

"Um Ally, are you alright?"

"Yeah, I'm fine. But you'll never believe what Miss Smith told me after class."

"What did she tell you?"

"She wants me to welcome some gifted kid to our school, because 'I could learn from him.'"

"Oh my god."

"I know, right? She's basically calling me stupid."

"Yeah, if you need help with school, you can just come to me", says Eliza.

"I know. The whole thing is so annoying."

After school, mom drives us home. She's driving in silence, until she finally drops the question.

"So Alyssa, anything you want to talk to me about?

Her words echo through my mind. Has she found the blades? Or my journal? My whole mind goes blank. There's only one word: Deny. Deny. Deny.

"Nope", I reply, trying to sound as casual as possible.

"Maybe about the new student transferring to your school tomorrow?"

Good, at least she didn't find anything in my room. I really don't want to tell her about the new kid, though. I've never been a very talkative person, not even as a child. That's why I only have one friend, Eliza. It's always been like that; I don't want it to change. I hate change.

If I tell her that there is a new student that I'm showing around, she's going to get all excited for me, even though he will probably abandon me as soon as

16

possible. But she obviously already knows something about it. I don't want to get in trouble for lying.

"Oh yeah, Miss Smith wants me to show him around and stuff", I say.

"Well that's great! I'm really happy that you're finally talking to others your age. I heard he's really smart, perhaps he could even help you with school!"

There it is.

"Maybe…"

That night, I'm sitting in my room doing my homework, in protest to what everyone is saying about my grades. I can't really seem to get much done, though. My mind is flooded with all kinds of emotions. I look in the mirror. I disgust myself. No wonder Eliza's friends looked at me like that. I would react the same way. I start crying, soundlessly. I'm pathetic. I open the drawer again and pull out the blade. I start cutting. I feel better for every cut that I make. I suddenly hear a knock on the door.

"Can I come in?"

It's mom.

"I'm changing", I quickly reply.

"Okay, well I'm going to bed."

"Alright, love you!" I say.

"Love you too, honey, Good night."

I put the blade down. Fuck. I almost got caught. I wait for the cuts to stop bleeding before I put the blade back in the drawer and go to sleep.

I actually sleep soundly, and wake up well rested.

I get up and look in the mirror, open my makeup bag. I curl my eyelashes and put some mascara on. It's a good lash day today! That's a sign, right? I put some deodorant on and get dressed in a cute sweater along with a pair of grey jeans. I actually look kind of cute today. This is the most confident I've felt in a long time. I go down for breakfast, and find my mom stressed as usual.

"Annie, have you seen my work ID?"

"No."

"Have you seen it, Alyssa?" she asks, not even looking at me.

"I haven't", I reply while buttering a piece of toast.

She lifts a pile of papers and sighs.

"Found it."

I roll my eyes, but can't help smiling. I love her no matter how disorganised she is.

When we're all ready, mom drives us to school as usual. During the whole ride I can't stop thinking about who this new kid is. I mean, all I know is that his name is Theodore and that he's gifted. I'm starting to panic. What if he hates me?

We arrive at school, and mom stops the car.

"Have a good day, kids."

"You too, mom", I say.

"Oh, and Alyssa. Be nice to the new kid."

"Love you too, mom", I sigh, and slam the car door. Mom drives off, and I walk straight into what I believe is a brand new day of misery.

In the big hall, Eliza runs up to me, and hugs me right away when she sees me.

"What was that for?" I ask.

"Just feel kind of bad for you, that's all".

"Haha", I reply with a straight face. "Maybe he'll be nice to me".

"Excuse me", says a voice behind me.

I turn around to see who it is. It's a tall, brown haired boy with glasses and dimples.

"Are you Alyssa?"

"Yes?"

"Theodore." He holds his hand out.

I can't think of a thing to say.

Chapter 2

Theo

Theodore? This is the gifted kid who just transferred? I was expecting some geeky guy, but this one is actually really cute. I scan him from head to toe. He's wearing a t-shirt and a flannel. I'm guessing it's a band t-shirt, but I don't recognize the band. He's also wearing baggy jeans and a pair of matt Doc Martens. There's a big birthmark on his neck, and the brown hair is really messy. But not in the way that would give you the impression that he's unorganised.

His dark eyes look right into mine. He's still holding his hand out and I finally take it.

"Nice to meet you", I say.

He looks at me curiously. But not in a disgusted way, like Eliza's friends do. More in a fascinated way, that really catches my attention.

"You're very beautiful", he suddenly blurts out.

At first I think he's looking at Eliza. But he's still looking right at me, and I just stand there, not knowing what to say or do. Eliza witnesses me just staring at him like an idiot. She hits my arm. I figure that's code for: "Say something, you dumb fuck."

"Thank you", I manage to reply.

He finally lets go of my hand, his facial expression suddenly changing. He looks really embarrassed as he stands there, with his mouth open like he's trying to say something.

"I-I was in Miss Smith's office earlier this morning", he stutters. "She told me to look for you. She gave me your name and a description. I'm not a creep or anything."

That explains the facial expression. He thought his comment made him come off as creepy. Eliza gives Theodore a slightly judgemental look.

"Uh huh", she says sarcastically.

Normally I would give Eliza a look clearly telling her to be nice, but the guy actually seems relieved by her words. He might not understand her sarcasm. I quickly think of a change of subject.

"Sooo.. what made you transfer here?"

"I moved here recently because of my dad's job. I'm from Sweden", Theodore replies.

Eliza and I look at him, and then at each other. He really doesn't look very Swedish at all. Swedish people are known for blonde hair and blue eyes.

"I'm half Swedish, half British", he adds.

It's almost like he read my mind.

"Anyway," I say. "We still have time before classes start, would you like a tour of the school?"

"For sure!"

I show Theodore around, and literally every time I say anything he replies with: 'Hmm, interesting' or 'Very nice'. He really isn't annoying or mean. He is actually nice. I don't hate him.

After the tour we go to class. We're quite early, even after walking around the whole school. Miss Smith tells Theodore to sit next to me. That, I do not like. We have desks for two in our classroom, and I used to be the only one in class who didn't have to share. But there are no other seats available, so I have to accept my new neighbour.

English is boring as usual, so I zone out, as usual. I'm doing alright in my own little world, when Theodore taps my shoulder.

"What?" I whisper, annoyed.

He slips me a note. It says: 'I heard you needed help with studies.' I look back at him, shaking my head. He grabs the note and starts scribbling something else, then hands it back to me. 'Everyone needs help sometimes.' I open my pencil case and write back: 'My grades aren't the best, but you really don't have to help me.' I hand him the note. He reads it, smiling the whole time, kind of like a psychopath. Then he picks up his pencil and starts writing again. I was hoping he would just accept that I don't want help, but apparently not. He hands me the note back.

'I want to', it says.

I look up at him. He's smiling at me, but not in a psychopath way anymore, but in a genuine way. I smile back at him. I pick up my pencil and write 'Thank you' on the note, and hand it to him. Theodore reads it, and then looks at me. We share a nod.

He just kind of follows me throughout the day. We have all the same classes, so it's convenient. We don't talk that much, just a bit of casual small talk. At the end of the day he comes up to me and starts talking about study plans.

"I want you to study for at least fifteen minutes every day", he says. "And meet with me once a week to study together."

"Study together? Why?" I ask, genuinely curious.

"Solo studies are important, but it's even more important to study with others to compare work and learn from each other."

I'm silent. I doubt he could learn anything from me, but I don't question him. He notices my silence, realising that I don't have any more questions.

"So on which week days can we meet?" he asks.

"Any of them, except Fridays."

Friday is an important day for me. It's when me and Eliza go to her house and watch movies. House isn't exactly the right word, her place is so huge it's practically a mansion. Also, her room is an ensuite with a massive walk-in closet. She really needs that closet though, because she has so many clothes. Her room is filled with all kinds of things. When we were younger, she had a large cardboard cut-out of Justin Bieber and expensive dolls in there, but now it's just makeup and other similar stuff. It's a part of growing up, I guess. Sometimes I'll sleep over there, in my own room. The guest rooms are like hotel rooms, complete with small bottles of shampoo and conditioner in the shower.

"How about Wednesdays?" Theodore asks. "Can you study then?"

"Yes, that'll be just fine."

"Great. Let's start next week."

"Thank you, Theodore."

"You could just call me Theo, if you'd like."

"Alright. I'll see you tomorrow, Theo."

When I come home that day, mom keeps asking me questions about Theo. I reply with 'I don't know' most of the time. Partly because I really DON'T know, and partly because I don't want to answer. She eventually stops asking, once she's realised I'm not going to answer her. She is really excited about me getting to know Theo. I don't want her to be. I mean, it's exciting that he's my second "friend" ever, but it won't be exciting once he leaves me.

"He's going to give up on you, once he realises what a freak you are. A monster. Not even worth to look at", says the voices in my head. I try not to listen to them, and turn on music instead. It works surprisingly well. I don't cut myself that night, even though I feel the need to. My wrists are sore enough anyway.

Theo keeps following me around school, and I'm getting to know him better. He's actually really nice. He and Eliza also get to know each other better, and she eventually ends up warming up to him. Eliza's other friends don't like him, though. They treat him like a male version of me. Dirty looks, whispers, but Theo doesn't seem bothered at all. It's like he doesn't even notice. He's only been here for a week, and people are already talking about him. Poor boy. Eliza doesn't seem to notice either - if she would, I'd expect her to say something.

Wednesday comes around, the day me and Theo will be studying together. I have been studying fifteen minutes every day for the past week, but I still feel nervous. The day goes by really fast. After school, Theo takes me to his house.

"Here it is."

I laugh, the house is huge! Massive even. It's a palace, bigger than Eliza's house. He must be joking. If he's that rich and smart, why is he even in public school?

"Why are you laughing?"

He's not joking. This really is his place.

"Oh, nothing", I say.

We go inside, and upstairs to Theo's room. It doesn't seem like his parents are home. His room is about the same size as mine, quite tiny for a house this big. There's a desk, a large bookshelf, a smaller bed, a wardrobe and an acoustic guitar in one of the corners.

Theo immediately empties his bag, not on the desk but on the floor. He sits down on the floor and just looks at me, smiling a little wickedly. I sit down next to him.

"So, tell me, what have you been studying the past week?" he asks.

"I've been working on the home economics exam and the German homework."

"So have I. Have you been studying for fifteen minutes every day like I asked?"

"Yes."

He sounds like a dad. I don't like it, but I don't have the nerve to tell him. I'm getting a weird vibe from him right now.

"Do you see any progress?"

"Kind of."

"Great! Let's get to studying then, shall we?"

We're doing homework for at least an hour. I lose track of time. Theo is truly as smart as they say he is. He seems to really enjoy school work. By the time we finish I feel prepared for school, both the exam and the homework. Theo is almost like a magician when it comes to this kind of stuff.

"Anything else you want to look at?" he asks me.

"Not really."

I look at his guitar. I used to play a few years ago. I wasn't too good, though. In the corner of my eye, I notice Theo looking at it as well.

"You play?" I ask.

"Yes! Want me to play something?"

"If you want to."

Theo gets up and grabs the guitar. He starts playing a melody that I never heard before. It's the most perfect indie rock song, not typically what I listen to, but I love it. He looks at peace while playing.

"What song is that?"

"Something I wrote. It still needs a bit of work, perhaps I'll add some lyrics."

He wrote that on his own? Jesus Christ, this guy is talented. I look at my phone, the time says five forty-seven PM.

"I've got to go", I say. "Thanks again."

"No worries. Same time next week?"

"Sure."

I gather my things and go home. I suddenly feel confident. I'm going to ace that test and that homework. And I actually can't wait to see Theo again, and listen to his music.

Chapter 3

Secret tampon

"... And then he played the most beautiful melody I've ever heard."

"Really, the most beautiful one?"

It's Friday, and I'm sleeping over at Eliza's place as usual. We just finished a movie, and now we're just gossiping. I'm telling her about my study session with Theo.

"Yes. He's really talented and rich, but his room is like… empty."

"So this rich, smart and talented guy just shows up at our school without explanation?"

"It's weird, right?

"Yeah. If I was him, I'd go to private school."

"Exactly. And I can't forget about his room being so small and empty."

Eliza's face suddenly lights up. I can sense that she has a bad idea.

"Show me where he lives," she laughs.

"Are you crazy? What if he sees us?"

"He's too nice to say something. Besides, if anything, he'll let us in, and I could see his empty room!"

I sigh. I really can't say no to this girl.

"Alright. But if he sees us, we pretend that we're just passing by."

"Sure!"

We put on our coats and walk over to Theo's huge house. The cold spring breeze is up in my face the whole time. Still feels like winter is in the air.

I stop in front of the house.

"This is it."

"This?" Eliza laughs. "I thought this was a school."

I look at the house. It does look like a school. Eliza looks at the house too, visibly intrigued.

"So, you mean to tell me that Theo lives in a small room in this huge place?"

"Weird, right?"

At that very moment, the front door opens. No no no, this can't be happening. Theo comes out holding a trash bag. He stops when he sees us. Eliza and I are frozen.

"Alyssa? Eliza? What are you two doing here?" he asks us, while dropping the trash bag into the dustbin.

"Um… We were just heading to the gas station to buy some soft drinks", Eliza says.

"Well, I have plenty inside, want to come in?"

"Thanks, but I think we're good…" I start replying.

"Yes please!" Eliza interrupts.

I give her a look but follow her inside anyway. The house is as cold as last time I was here, but at least it's warmer than outside. Theo looks at Eliza, who is wearing a skirt.

"You must be freezing", he says to her.

"Oh, I'm fine."

"Nonsense. Come on, let's go to my room."

Eliza grins at me and follows him up the stairs. I follow too. Theo's bedroom looks almost as empty as I remembered. There's now an electric guitar next to the acoustic one. Theo opens the wardrobe, searching for something. Meanwhile, Eliza curiously looks around the room.

"Shit, Ally. You were right", she whispers.

"Here it is!" Theo suddenly turns up from the wardrobe. He's holding a pair of girl's jeans. Why would he have those? He hands them to Eliza.

"Size small?" he asks her.

"Yes. How did you know?"

"My mom is a fashion designer. She taught me how to measure these things when I was a kid, so I have an excellent eye measurement."

Eliza says nothing.

"The bathroom is right next to my room if you want to change."

Theo points to a small door inside his room. I hadn't noticed that door before.

"Thanks."

Eliza leaves the room. Theo looks at me, smiling ear to ear.

"Notice anything different?" he asks.

I look at his guitars.

"You have an electric guitar now."

"Yes! and you'll love this."

Theo walks over to the desk, opens his laptop and types in a sketchy website. It's a music creator. He presses play on an untitled song. It's the same melody that he played Wednesday, with drums and bass added, and well, everything! How did he manage to create all of that in such a short amount of time? It's literally a three-minute song.

"It's kind of messy still", he says. "It's not finished, it needs some perfecting and perhaps some lyrics."

"Messy?!" I say, louder than I intended. "I've played music before, but I've never seen someone that can create a masterpiece this quickly!

"Oh, you've played music before, huh? Interesting."

"Yes, I used to do a bit of singing."

"Perfect. Perhaps you could help me with the song, then."

I'm just about to tell him that it is a terrible idea, and how bad I am at singing, when Eliza returns.

"She would love to!" she says.

"Great! You look good in those pants by the way, Eliza."

"Thanks for letting me borrow them. Now, let's talk about soft drinks!"

We go downstairs, and while Eliza is looking around in Theo's fridge, Theo is asking me questions about singing.

"How long have you been singing for?"

"First of all, I don't sing anymore. I did for about four years, when I was younger."

"Four years? You must have a lot of experience, then."

"Not exactly."

"Well, I still would like you to sing my song, it'll be fun! First of all, it would help us get to know each other. Secondly, I really want to add a feminine voice into the song."

"Alright then, let's do it."

"Super. I'll let you know when I have some lyrics."

"Sounds good."

Theo and I suddenly hear a long gasp leaving Eliza's mouth.

"You have marble drinks?" She yelps, holding a lychee flavoured one.

"Yes! It's one of my favourites", Theo replies.

"Oh my God, mine too, and Ally's. Where did you get these?"

"I got them from a Japanese website."

"Wait, really?" Eliza says in disbelief. "That must be so expensive, especially with shipping included."

"My parents like to reward my good grades."

"That's correct", a strange woman's voice suddenly says behind us.

This must be Theo's mom. She walks into the kitchen.

"I wish you would have talked to me before inviting your friends, but I guess it's fine."

"Allow me to introduce you to them", Theo says. "This is Alyssa and Eliza."

"Right, so which one of you is being tutored by my son?"

I say nothing. Theo's mom is very intimidating. She's tall and blonde, and the way she speaks with a very blank facial expression, makes her seem scary. I don't have to say anything though, because Eliza is pointing right at me. She's probably intimidated by this woman as well. Theo's mom nods at me.

"Right. I have to get back to work", she tells us while taking a beer out from the fridge. "Have fun, okay?"

I sigh in relief. Theo's mom was very close to making my heart stop.

"Your mom seems cool", Eliza says.

"Yeah, she's alright."

We each grab a soft drink and go into 'the tv room' as Theo refers to it. The tv room is huge, it's more of a home movie theatre.

"Ally!" Eliza scream-whispers. "You didn't tell me that this guy had his own movie theatre."

"I didn't know!"

"Didn't know what?" Theo asks.

"Nothing!"

We begin browsing through movies. Theo finds one that looks quite interesting.

"A romcom! Interesting choice", I say.

"No", Eliza protests. "I hate romcoms, they're so boring. I want to watch a thriller."

"Sorry, Elz. It's two against one."

"Aw, shit."

Theo turns the movie on, and it's actually really boring. Eliza was right. Twenty minutes in, she falls asleep on my shoulder. I giggle a bit before wrapping my arm around her. Theo seems to be really into the movie. He's watching, with an incredibly fascinated facial expression. He's such a nerd. I move a little closer to him. He looks at me, and then at Eliza. He starts laughing.

"When did Eliza fall asleep?"

"I don't know. She just started leaning very heavily on my shoulder."

"That's cute."

Fortunately, the movie is quite short. It feels like it's just getting more and more boring. I can't be happier when it's over.

"Elz, wake up."

"What?"

"It's getting late, and we've got to go home."

"Right."

Theo shows us to the door.

"You can keep those pants by the way, Eliza."

"Really? But they're so nice."

"I don't need them."

"That's really sweet of you, Theo", I say. "Come on, let's go now, I'm tired."

We leave. The whole way home, Eliza is talking about how great Theo is. I think he won her over with the marble drinks, but I'm not telling her that.

"Even though he seems to be a great guy, something about him still doesn't sit well with me", Eliza concludes.

"What?"

She takes something out of her pocket. It's... a tampon? She's holding it in her hand, looking at me with big eyes.

"What the fuck is this?" I ask.

"It was in Theo's bathroom."

"You stole from him?" I shout.

"I just thought it was suspicious and wanted to show it to you."

"That doesn't give you the right to steal!"

Eliza stares at the tampon. She looks upset. Why did I do it, why did I yell at my best friend? My ONLY friend. I suck.

"I'm sorry, Elz. I didn't mean that."

"It's fine, I mean, I shouldn't have stolen. I just thought it was so strange that he would have those."

"Maybe they're for his sister, or his girlfriend", I sigh.

"If he had a sister, there would be pictures of her everywhere, right? And there's just no way that a guy like him has a girlfriend."

I look at the tampon. It seems kind of strange that he has it. I look at Eliza. She's waiting for me to say something.

"Let's just go."

Eliza nods, and we go back to her place.

Chapter 4

Song

I'm lying in my bed, doing my daily fifteen minutes of studying. I'm going to Theo's tomorrow, and I want to impress him with my newly found study skills. I'm so tired, though. Part of me wants to sleep forever and never wake up.

The doorbell rings suddenly.

"Can you get that, Alyssa?" Mom yells from downstairs.

I sigh and go downstairs. Whoever is ringing is doing it multiple times. Jesus Christ. I open the door and it's…

"Theo?!"

"I have it! I have it, Al!" he says, smiling from ear to ear.

Did he just call me Al? How did he know where I live? And what does he have?

"I'm sorry, what?"

"The lyrics!"

"Lyrics?"

"To my song! Pay attention, Al!"

"Can't this wait until tomorrow?"

"I'm afraid it cannot."

Suddenly I get a feeling that someone is standing behind me. I turn around, and there's mom.

"You must be Theodore", she says in a cheerful voice. "It's a pleasure to finally meet you."

"Oh, don't mind me", Theo says. "I'm just here to propose an idea to your daughter."

"Okay. You kids go have fun, but not too much fun."

"Thanks mom", I say, grabbing Theo's arm and pulling him up the stairs.

I only let go of him when we reach my room. I stare at him, angrily.

"You look upset", he says. "What's going on?"

"How did you find my address?"

"Eliza gave it to me."

"So, you call her Eliza and not El?"

"Why would I call her El?"

"Because you just called me Al!?"

"Right", he says, slowly and sceptically.

I scoff. We were scheduled to meet tomorrow, not right now. Well, I suppose since he's here, we might as well take a look at the lyrics he wrote.

"Sorry for being so intense", I say. "Can I see the lyrics, then?"

Theo's face lights up.

"For sure."

He takes out a couple of paper sheets from his bag and hands them to me. I look. "Battery is running low", it's called. The lyrics tell a tale about a person with low energy, trying to find someone who can make them happy and "recharge them". I really relate to this text. It seems so unique, too.

"What do you think?"

"They're perfect", I say. "I've never seen anything like it. I love it!"

He grins at me.

"That's great! So, you'll sing it with me, then?"

I nod. His smile gets even wider, and he pulls me in for a big hug.

"Thank you, Al."

He lets go of me, and can I feel my smile fading.

"Are you okay?" Theo asks me.

I stay silent for a second, not knowing what to say. I look away from him.

"Do you believe in me?" I ask him.

"What kind of question is that? Of course, I do."

"Really?"

"Absolutely. Now, let me hear you sing."

"What should I sing?"

"Anything you want."

I close my eyes. I'm beginning to sing. I'm singing Eliza's favourite song, 'Sweater Weather' by The Neighbourhood. It's been her favourite song for years. Since it means a lot to her, it means a lot to me too. I open my eyes again. Theo's staring at me with his mouth wide open.

"Wow, you sing way better than me", he says.

"Shut up!" I laugh.

"No but seriously, you have major talent. I can't believe we'll be working together!"

"It'll be fun."

"Can I ask you something?"

I nod.

"What did your mom mean by 'have fun, but not too much fun'? Doesn't she want us to have fun?"

I laugh, he's obviously joking. He's not laughing with me.

"She just doesn't want us to fool around."

"Like, get into trouble?"

"No. I mean yes, but that's not what she meant."

He looks at me in a strange way.

"She doesn't want us to... you know, have…"

"Have what?"

"... Have sex."

"Why would we do that? It's not like we are interested in procreation."

"That's not the only reason people have sex, you know."

"Anyway, I've got to go. Keep the music sheets, I have many copies at home."

"Oh okay, should I see you to the…"

"No, I'll be fine", he says, already running downstairs with a flustered look on his face.

"Theo, wait…"

"See you tomorrow, Al!"

I don't even bother running after him, I just stand in my room like an idiot. He's probably just embarrassed. I hear the front door closing, followed by footsteps coming up the stairs. Before I know it, mom is standing in my room.

"Why did Theodore leave so soon?" I didn't even have time to make tea."

"I don't know."

"Well, what did you two talk about?"

"Nothing."

I hide the music sheets behind my back.

"Let me see that."

She snatches the sheets from me and starts reading through them.

"Hey, give that back!" I shout.

"What is this?"

I sigh.

"It's something me and Theo are working on. It's a song."

"Oh that's fun, what's your part?"

"I sing."

She lights up in a big smile.

"That's lovely. I'm so happy for you, honey! It's been a while since I heard you sing."

"It has, hasn't it?"

The next day Eliza and I are talking about Theo again.

"Regardless of why he had that… thing, he's a great guy and I should apologise for stealing", Eliza concludes.

"Yeah… or, you should not tell him about it at all. After all, he doesn't seem to have noticed."

"How would you know that?"

"Well, he didn't mention it when he came to my house yesterday."

"Oh yeah, I forgot. He told me in gym class that he wanted to surprise you and needed your address."

"So you just gave him my address, then?"

"M-hm! What was the surprise?"

"Well… We are working on that song together, the one that he played for me the other day? And he showed me the lyrics."

"Oh, you're working on a song? Well, if you ever need a pianist, I'm right here."

"We'd love to have you, Eliza!" a cheerful voice says behind me.

I turn around and see Theo with the signature dimple smile on his face.

"How long have you been standing there?" I ask in shock.

"Long enough to know that Eliza wants to help us with our little project."

"I'd love to help!"

"Then it's settled, the three of us are now officially a band. How would you like to have your Friday sleepover at my house? You'll get your own rooms, if you're more comfortable that way."

"That sounds like fun!" Eliza says. "We'll work on the song then?"

"Yes! However, right now we should probably get to class."

Chapter 5

Caught

I step into the shower. The hot water makes my scars burn, and I forget everything. I forget about my wish to die. It's a quick shower though, since I'm soon going over to Theo's for the sleepover. I studied the lyrics last night, and now I pretty much know the whole song by heart.

When I'm all set and ready to go, the doorbell rings. I open the door for Eliza.

"Hey, Elz, what are you doing here? Aren't we supposed to meet at Theo's?"

"I kind of forgot where he lives", she says, giggling. "Can we go together?"

"Of course we can."

Mom enters the hallway.

"Oh hello, Eliza. I wasn't expecting you two to have your sleepover here. I thought you were going to Theodore's."

"Hey, Mrs Tucker! I just thought Ally and I could go together."

"Oh, I see. Have fun, okay?"

"We will", I reply while tying my shoelaces. "Bye, mom."

I swiftly walk out the front door, and Eliza follows. We walk to Theo's house. It's only a fifteen-minute walk, but it feels longer. When we get there, Theo's mom lets us in.

"Theo! The girls are here", she shouts.

Theo turns up, wearing sweatpants and a hoodie. It looks really good on him. But I would never tell him that.

"Hey girls, are you ready to work on this thing?"

"I was born ready!" Eliza exclames, stepping inside.

I just nod a little, hesitantly walking behind her.

"The music room is right downstairs", Theo says, as if having a dedicated music room is the most casual thing ever.

Eliza and I look at each other, slightly shocked.

"Music room?!" We shout simultaneously.

"Come on, I'll show you."

Theo leads us to a door by the staircase, leading into the basement. The basement has several rooms. It's like a maze, just like the rest of the house. He opens a door, revealing a fancy music room. The room is massive, filled with several instruments. Mainly guitars, but still. The inside of the room is decorated with neon lights and framed pictures of famous musicians. Some of the pictures are even signed.

" Oh shit, this is nice", Eliza blurts out.

"Yeah", I agree. "You must be really passionate about music, Theo."

"I am. But this is actually my dad's room, he's a musician."

"You don't say", I mumble.

"Anyways, I don't really know how skilled you are, Eliza. Would you care to play us something?"

"Sure! Ally knows what I like to play", she says, looking at me with a sly smile. "Would you like to join in? It's been so long since I heard you sing."

I stop to think for a moment. Everything in me wants to say no, but after all, this is the main reason why I'm here.

"Yes, I'll join."

I care too much about Eliza to be an ass about it. I know which song she wants to play, and how much she loves that song. Without a doubt, she's thinking about the same song I sang to Theo. Eliza sits down at the keyboard and starts playing effortlessly. I close my eyes and sing the best I can. I mess up a few times, but Eliza of course plays flawlessly.

"Wow, Ally", she says when we're finished. "That was really good."

"Thanks, but you did better."

"You both did great", Theo says.

"Thanks. I've actually never heard you play?" There's a suggestion in Eliza's voice.

"Right." Theo picks up one of the guitars and plays a few chords, equally as effortless as Eliza. She looks really impressed. I'm also watching him play in pure admiration. It seems to be a very hard song to play, but he makes it look so easy. At one point, Eliza grabs my arm like she's about to fall over. I look at her and she has this shocked look on her face, but still with a large, heart-warming smile. As Theo finishes playing, it hits me. I'm completely talentless compared to him and Eliza.

"That was amazing", Eliza squeals.

"I know", he laughs. "No, but seriously, we've really got something here. With your incredible piano skills, my guitar playing and Al's strong voice, we could be great together."

'Al's strong voice?' I feel a smile forming on my face, and butterflies roaming about in my stomach. I guess it's natural. Everyone likes compliments, especially from someone more talented than themselves.

"No question", I say.

"I actually have something to tell the both of you", Eliza suddenly says.

"What is it?" Theo asks, excitedly.

"I'm organising a school event. A talent show, to be more specific. Maybe we could enter with your song, Theo."

My heart starts beating faster. Performing, in front of people? I'm suddenly getting nervous. I can't really protest, though.

"Honestly, that would be so much fun", Theo says. "It's the perfect opportunity to show off our work."

"Sounds like a lot of pressure, but I'm willing to give it a go", I cautiously agree.

"Oh, thank you, Ally!" Eliza looks so happy.

We practise Theo's song all night. Eliza needs the most practice, since she's only getting familiar with the song. She plays well, though, and Theo does too. I find myself feeling kind of unimportant tonight. They're so great, and I'm just me.

"I'm really tired, we should probably leave it here for now", I say after a few hours.

"Same", Eliza agrees.

"I could show you to your rooms, if you'd like", Theo offers.

Eliza looks at me, and then at Theo.

"I've been thinking. Us all sleeping in separate rooms kind of ruins the whole 'sleepover experience'."

"So you guys would like to sleep in my room?"

"If Ally wants to."

They both look at me.

"Sure, I guess."

Shit, I wasn't expecting this to happen. I only brought a short sleeve shirt to sleep in. I feel like crying.

"Are you okay, Ally?" Eliza asks me.

"I'm fine. Just tired."

A few minutes later, I'm in Theo's bathroom panicking. What am I going to do? I can't walk out in short sleeves, or they'll see my scars. I decide to just wear the long sleeve and pretend it's all I have. I step out and Eliza gives me a look almost instantly. Theo isn't in the room.

"Where's Theo?" I ask.

"He's making us noodles. What are you wearing?"

"What do you mean?"

"I know that you have a blue t-shirt in your bag. I saw it."

"I'm freezing", I lie.

"You can't be. I'm always freezing, and I'm warm right now."

I feel the tears coming, and next thing I know, I'm ugly crying. Eliza stares at me, stunned, before running up to hug me.

"I'm so sorry, Ally. I didn't mean to make your cry!"

"It's not you."

I roll up my sleeve, revealing dozens of scars.

"I didn't want you to know. I didn't want anyone to know."

"Oh, Ally! I don't know what to say... I'm so sorry."

I continue to cry in Eliza's arms, until I hear someone entering the room.

"What did you do to your arm?"

It's Theo. He's holding a big plate of instant noodles.

"I-I..."

"Don't worry, I understand", he interrupts.

He puts the plate down on the floor and joins our hug.

"I didn't want anyone to know, but now that you two know, I feel better", I finally sob.

"You can trust us, we won't say a thing", Eliza says.

"That may be true, but I still strongly suggest that you get some professional help", says Theo.

"Well. For now, I think some instant noodles could do the trick."

"Yes ma'am, Theo says, smiling.

He goes over to grab the noodles, and I return to the bathroom, to finally change into sleep wear.

When I get home the next day, I find mom and Annie sitting in the kitchen.

"Hi, Ally. Have a seat, we need to talk."

Chapter 6

More secrets

"Family therapy?!"

"Yes. Since clearly you're still not thinking straight after the death of your father", mom says.

"Oh, so this is all about me, then?"

"It's about the whole family, that's why it's called family therapy."

"I DO think straight!" I shout.

"Sure, it's not like your grades have dropped and you now need a tutor who does all the work for you."

"What?! Theo does NOT do all the work for me!"

"Well, regardless, the three of us are about to start family therapy again, and there's nothing you can do about it. Now go to your room!"

I stomp my way up to my room.

"Enough with the stomping, you're sixteen, start acting like it!"

As soon as I get into my room, I start crying. I hate the things I do. I don't want to go to family therapy. I don't want to go to therapy at all!

I open the drawer and take out one of my blades. I cut myself a few times before rolling my sleeves back down.

Shortly after, I hear mom outside my door. Fuck.

"Obviously you're grounded", she says as she enters.

"But you're already punishing me with this whole family therapy thing."

"Do you think that I'm paying 200 pounds an hour for your punishment? This is about healing."

Perhaps she's right. Dad's death has been hard on us all, and even though I didn't like therapy last time, it doesn't mean I'll hate it this time.

"I'm sorry", I say quietly. "I'll go to therapy."

"It's not like you have a choice, young lady. But it feels good that you want to go."

Mom gives me a hug, and I feel tears in my eyes. I don't know why I'm tearing up, I just am.

"You're still grounded until next weekend", mom says.

"That's fine."

Days go by, and everything is kind of fine. My punishment is that I can't go out for a week, but since I just like to stay in, I don't suffer too much. Until Wednesday, that is.

"What do you mean, I can't go to my study session?"

"It's a part of your punishment."

"But I have a big math test tomorrow!"

"Please, Alyssa. I saw you study yesterday. You'll pass, I'm sure."

"No, because studying together is the most important part. Sure, solo studies are important, but studying together allows us to compare our work and learn from each other."

I realise that I directly quoted Theo. Maybe we're more alike than I thought.

"Um, okay then. I guess Theodore is welcome to come over."

My blood starts to boil. I can't have him at my house right now, it's a mess!

"Now you're just being ridiculous, I can't even study at a friend's house?"

"It's either that, or nothing."

"Fine!"

I go up to my room to ring Theo. Mom doesn't stop me.

I pick up my phone and dial his number. He takes a while to respond.

"Hi, Al. Where are you? Are you sick?"

"No but I am grounded."

"I see, so you can't come over."

"Sadly no, I'm sorry."

"That's okay."

"Mom did say that you could come over if you'd like. I just can't come to you."

"Okay, I'll be there! I could bring you some snacks if you want, you know, to cheer you up."

A smile spreads on my face. He'd really do that for me? He's so sweet.

"Thank you. That would be nice."

"Anytime, Al. I'll be there right away."

He hangs up the phone without saying goodbye. I immediately go downstairs to let mom know that he is on his way. She tells me that she's proud of me for listening. Silently I'm thinking that she really shouldn't be, listening is the bare minimum I can do.

Twenty minutes later, Theo is ringing the doorbell. I open the door and stare into a huge paper bag that he's holding.

"Hi!" Theo exclaims.

"Hi", mom's voice says behind me.

She all of a sudden seems to be in a good mood. She walks up to us, smiling weirdly.

"Hello, Mrs Tucker", Theo greets her. "You must excuse my bad manners, but I have a question "

Oh no. What now?

"That's alright Theodore, ask away."

"Why is Al grounded?"

Fuck, this guy really has no filter. Mom looks flabbergasted. She really wasn't expecting that. I realise what Theo is doing from the grin on his face. He's asking on purpose, probably to make her feel a bit bad. I usually don't know if he does certain things on purpose, but this time it's pretty clear.

"She just made some bad choices", mom explains, after collecting herself. "Everyone makes mistakes. Right, Alyssa?"

"Right", I reply.

"Right", Theo says.

"Anyway, I better get the vacuum out. You kids have fun comparing your work and learning from each other."

Why did she have to say it like that?

"We will, mom."

I pull Theo upstairs by the arm.

"You've got to stop doing that", he says when we're in my room.

I silence him with a tight hug. "Thank you."

He hugs me back.

"You're welcome. I wouldn't want anyone to hurt you, and when I found out that you…"

He pulls away from me and starts whispering.

"…would do, that, to yourself… I just wanted to stop it somehow, and I figured standing up for you would be the first step."

I start to tear up, reminded of everything that hurts.

"I just want you to know that you can always talk to me, no matter what", Theo adds.

Tears run down my face. I feel like I'm about to explode, and then I do.

"My dad died last year", I blurt out.

I start sobbing aggressively. I'm looking down at the floor, so I can't see Theo's face. I'm sure he looks very surprised. Then, I suddenly feel him wrap his arms around me.

"Shh, it's alright, Al", he reassures me.

His voice sounds so calming. I look up at him. He's looking back at me. He wipes away my tears, then leans in to kiss me. I let him. It's a nice, soothing kiss. It really makes me feel better, somehow. It would be even better if I couldn't hear mom vacuuming downstairs. He pulls away from me, his face gets all red.

"I'm sorry", he says.

I scoff. "For what?"

We share another kiss.

"That makes me feel better", I say, smiling.

"Look, I know we don't know each other that well, but will you be my…"

He hesitates. I look up at him waiting for him to say the magical word. The G word.

"… Girlfriend?"

"Yes, Theo. I feel like we connect so well."

"Really? Wow, that makes me so happy! I can't believe you're my first girlfriend."

"And actually, you're my first boyfriend."

"Oh? That's cool, Al. However, there's something about me that you should know…"

Something I should know? His facial expression changes from pure happiness to… worry?

"I'm… transgender."

Transgender? I try to collect my thoughts. He's a girl?

I feel so bad now. I have been calling her 'he' all this time.

"You're a girl? Um, that's alright. I support you."

"What? No!" he exclaims in a high-pitched voice. "I'm a guy. I was born a girl."

"Oh God, sorry! I thought you were male to female."

"Why would you think that?" He looks horrified. "I'm not. I told my parents early, and they supported my transformation. But then I got bullied so badly for being trans, we had to move away. So, we came here from Sweden, for me to get a fresh start."

"That really sucks, I'm so sorry. But I'll accept you no matter who you were in your past."

I put my arms around him. He wipes away tears from his face.

"Thanks, Al. I had to tell you; I think Eliza is on to me."

"Really? Why do you think that?"

"Well, before I started hormone therapy, I still had my period every month. I kept the tampons in my bathroom, in case mom would need some extra. I think Eliza found them. And then there were the jeans…"

He knows. My heart skips a beat. I can't rat out Eliza, though.

"Well, I've known Elz my whole life and if she did know, I'm sure that she would accept you. And if you ever need someone to talk to about it, I'm always here."

"Thank you. Sweden is actually one of the safest countries for trans people, but the small town I lived in was horrible."

A few years ago, a classroom in Västerköping, Sweden.

"Well done on the test, Thea. 100% again!"

"Thanks, but my name is Theodore. I even wrote it down on the test".

"How many times do I have to tell you? You are a girl, and your name is Thea. You are not a boy, and your name is not Theodore."

"It is, and I am a boy!"

"Don't be silly! Now, go back to your seat."

"The teacher said that?!" I stare at Theo in disbelief.

My blood is practically boiling. How dare anyone say such things to Theo?!

"Yes, and the kids were even worse, of course."

"Hey, fake boy!"

"Me?"

"Yes, you! You're the only girl who thinks she's a boy. How are you so smart? Is the fake penis that your rich parents paid for the secret?"

"Theo, that's horrible. I'm so sorry."

"I know. Although I'm sure Eliza would accept me for being transgender, I just want to keep it low key for now."

"That's fine, I understand."

The evening goes by, and we don't study at all. We just lie on my bed, cuddling. He's opening up to me.

Chapter 7

Date night

"I'm so happy for you, Ally!" Eliza squeals.

"It's not a big deal."

"Not a big deal?! You've got your first boyfriend, Theo is really nice too, and smart!"

"Alyssa and Eliza, be quiet back there!" The teacher says in her strictest voice.

"Sorry", we say simultaneously.

We have Home Economics class, and Theo is sitting three rows in front of us. He's not paying attention, but I can't really blame him since we're not either. He's scribbling on a note, then hands it to the person behind him. A few people pass around the note until it reaches us. That's when we realise that it's actually two notes.

They're both neatly folded and on one of them it says "Alyssa and Eliza" and the other one just says "Al".

"Who wrote these?" Eliza whispers to me.

I look at the "Al" note. Yes, definitely written by Theo.

"Let's just open them."

We open the one with both our names first.

We may need to practise more before the talent show. Would you like to meet in the music room after school?

"Sounds good!" Eliza says.

"Yes! I'm not grounded anymore, so I can go."

Eliza gives Theo a discrete thumbs up, and he gives one back. Then he looks at me, and I realise that I've completely forgotten about the note right in front of me. I look down at it. "Al". I open it.

Would you like to go on a date Saturday night?

My heart starts beating faster and my face gets hot. He just asked me out on a date! Obviously he was going to eventually, since he's my boyfriend, but it still brings butterflies to my stomach. I hear a sudden gasp leave Eliza's mouth, and I realise that she has been reading over my shoulder.

"You have to say yes", she begs excitedly.

"I'm going to!"

The bell rings and everyone gets up to leave. Eliza and I walk out together.

In the hall I see Theo, waiting for me. I look at Eliza, and she nods. I run up to Theo and hug his arm tightly.

"I would love to go on a date with you."

"Good", he giggles slightly. "I already booked us a table; I wouldn't want to sit there all alone."

Saturday comes around, and I start to realise that I have nothing to wear. I'm searching through my whole closet, but nothing good. Suddenly there's a knock on my bedroom door. It's mom, and Eliza is with her! Eliza is holding a plastic bag in her hand.

"Elz, what are you doing here?"

"You seriously thought I'd miss the chance of getting my best friend ready for her first date?"

"Alyssa, why didn't you tell me about your date with Theodore? I'm so happy for you!" Mom smiles.

"Sorry, but I really need to get ready now, Theo is picking me up in forty minutes!"

"Right, I'll leave you two to it."

Eliza comes into my room and closes the door. She turns the bag upside down and dumps all its contents on my bed. My jaw literally drops. Makeup and hair products, along with a really pretty mint green dress.

"I got these for you", she says. "I thought you might want to wear your own jewellery."

"Thanks, but you really didn't have to."

"Nonsense! It's your first date."

Did I ever mention that Eliza is really good at makeup? She starts doing mine, and when she's finished

I feel like a new person. It's nothing too dramatic, it's actually really subtle. But it still gives me a massive confidence boost.

"Wow, I love it!"

"It's probably my best work yet", Eliza says with great satisfaction. "Now, try on the dress I got you, I'll look away."

"You don't have to do that", I laugh.

"What?"

Shit, what do I say?

"I mean, we've known each other for ages, you don't have to look away."

Eliza nods, and I start taking my shirt off. Eliza doesn't look uncomfortable, even though I thought she might.

The dress fits perfectly. When I'm fully changed, Eliza moves on to my hair. She does a half-up-half-down style, and it looks really good. I tie the whole look together with my favourite earrings and a necklace that my dad gave me. I look in the mirror and gasp out loud. I can't believe how good I look!

"You did it", I say, admiring myself.

"Oh, Ally! He's going to love it!"

I turn to Eliza.

"You like it, right?"

"Of course I do. But you always look beautiful."

I give Eliza a long hug. Then the doorbell rings. I can hear Theo and mom talking downstairs.

"What are you waiting for?" Eliza asks. "Get down there, I'm right behind you."

I nod and start making my way towards the staircase. Theo is chatting with my mom, but he completely stops once he sees me coming down the stairs. He's wearing a white button-down shirt and a dark red tie, along with blue jeans and a pair of fancy shoes. He's holding a bouquet of pink and white roses, my two favourite colours. He looks shocked, but in a good way. He's kind of blushing, too. I realise that my face is turning red as well. We're both standing there, almost frozen. Eliza pushes me slightly, and I figure that's code for: 'go talk to him, you dumb fuck!'. So, I do.

"Hi, Theo."

'Hi, Theo'?! I'm going on a date with this guy, what do I mean 'hi'? His face melts into a smile, still blushing.

"Hi", he says. "You look really lovely. These are for you."

He hands me the bouquet.

"They're absolutely gorgeous. Thank you."

"I knew you'd like them, I asked Eliza about your favourite colours."

He looks at Eliza, who is still standing by the staircase. She raises her hands.

"Guilty as charged."

"Let me put those in some water", mom says, taking the flowers from my hands.

"Thanks, mom."

She leaves for the kitchen. I look at Eliza, she's looking at Theo. She nods at him.

"Should we go on our date, then?" Theo asks, a bit nervously.

I look at Eliza. I'm not sure I want to leave her here.

"You two have fun, I'll be okay", Eliza reassures me.

I cling on to Theo's arm and say bye to mom and Eliza. We walk out to Theo's car. Wait, he has a car? He opens the passenger door for me and I get in. It's a really nice car.

"Do you have a licence?" I ask him. It's a stupid question, but I can't help it. This is all very impressive.

"Yes, I actually just got it. Passed on the first try, of course." He grins at me.

"Not really surprised by that. But you have to have lived in the UK for at least 185 days, right?

"I have lived in the UK longer than that. I just did online school in the beginning, because I was scared."

He was scared? I hadn't even thought about that, even though it makes so much sense. Especially considering what happened to him in Sweden. I feel so stupid.

"I'm sorry, I didn't think."

"It's fine", he says, putting a gentle hand on my leg. "Don't let that ruin this night."

I smile at him, and he smiles back at me.

"Oh, and before I forget."

He reaches into the back seat and picks up a small paper bag. He takes out an even smaller box from the bag, and hands it to me.

"You got me another gift?"

"Only the best for you, Al."

"Thank you so much."

"Well, open it!"

I open the little box to reveal a bracelet with an infinity symbol charm attached to it. The charm is decorated with a few tiny diamonds. It's very cute.

"It's so pretty, Theo".

"Look at the back of the charm."

I take the bracelet out of the box and discover that there's something engraved on the back of the charm.

You will always be our Ally.

"It's beautiful. What happened to 'Al', though?"

"Well, the bracelet is from Eliza too, that's why it says '**our** Ally'."

He's looking down, with a nervous and embarrassed face expression. I lean over and kiss him on the cheek. He looks up at me and smiles.

"Let me help you put it on."

Theo puts the bracelet on, and the diamonds reflect the sunshine. He starts the car and drives towards the town's centre.

We have dinner at a very nice restaurant, and talk about our band practices. I even open up about going to family therapy. After dinner we drive down to the beach to watch the sunset. He parks the car in a spot where we can see the sun setting into the ocean. We get out of the car and sit on the front of it.

"This is so beautiful", I say.

"I know, right? Hey Al, I actually have one last gift for you."

"Really, one more?"

"Stay right here."

Theo gets off the car front, and reaches into the backseat. He takes out his acoustic guitar. Then he returns and sits right next to me again.

Theo clears his throat, then starts singing and playing. I suddenly realise he's singing about me. He's serenading. I can feel myself blushing. He's looking at me the whole time. It must be really hard, playing the guitar while focusing your eyes on something else. I think about all the practice he must have had. All just for me. He's so cute. I could watch him for hours, but he finishes the song after a couple of minutes.

"What do you think?"

"It's beautiful. Did you write that yourself?"

"Yeah, I wanted to show you how special you are. Even though we've only known each other a few weeks…"

The mood is suddenly ruined for me. Why did he have to bring up that we still hardly know each other?

And why is suddenly a feeling of guilt eating me up from inside?

"Yeah, well, it must be something special."

Moments later, he's taking me home. When we reach my house he walks me to the door.

"I had fun tonight", he says.

"Me too."

He leans in for a kiss, and I kiss him back. Something feels different, even though it's the same as Wednesday.

"Well, I'll see you on Monday", he says.

"Yeah, see you then. Bye. And thanks for everything."

I go inside and into the kitchen. There's Eliza, helping Annie with homework at the kitchen table. What?

"Eliza? What are you still doing here?"

"Oh, hi Ally! Your mom had a job emergency and had to come in. Since I was already here, I offered to look after Annie."

"She's helping me with math! Annie grins. "Multiplication is hard."

"So… how did the date go?" Eliza asks curiously.

"Yeah, I want to know too", says Annie.

I can feel my facial expression change. That weird feeling when Theo started talking about how we've only known each other for a short time, is coming back. Eliza looks at me with worried eyes. She turns to Annie.

"It's getting late. Why don't you go brush your teeth and get ready for bed, Annie?"

Annie looks disappointed, but leaves anyway. Eliza taps her empty seat. I sit down next to her.

"Was the date not what you expected?"

"No, I mean, it was great. He was great. But then he started talking about that we've only known each other for a short while, and it made me feel weird…"

Eliza looks confused.

"Why would he want to point that out? Does he want things to be weird?"

"I don't know, maybe he was just nervous. I really do like him, but… He's right. This is going very fast."

"No, yeah… but you should totally continue seeing him. No question."

She says it in such a weird way, almost like she doesn't want me to see him. But she's my best friend, and I have to trust that she means what she's saying. I know she only wants what's best for me.

"Thanks, Elz. I will."

Eliza gives me a weird looking smile.

"We should probably go check on Annie."

"Yeah, we should."

Chapter 8

Friends forever

"No, Eliza, you're doing it wrong!"

"Sorry! I just don't know how this thing works. I've played the piano my whole life. The first time I saw a man play guitar I was like 'where are the keys?'"

I'm standing in the doorway to the music room at school. Theo is trying to teach Eliza how to play the guitar. She really doesn't understand how to do it. The whole situation is quite humorous, at least from where I'm standing. Theo suddenly notices me. He instantly lights up.

"If it isn't my favourite girl!"

He walks up to me and kisses my cheek, and I giggle a bit. He's so charming. I look at Eliza. She's looking at us with a smile, but she also looks kind of sad.

"I was trying to teach Eliza how to play the guitar", Theo explains.

"I'm really good." Eliza laughs a little.

Theo gets a little closer to me. "She's not", he mumbles close to my ear.

"I heard that!"

I start laughing. Seems like they're really getting along. However, I can't help but wonder if Eliza is angry with me. She seems a little off.

"Anyway, we should probably practise a bit before it's time to lock up", I remind them.

Somehow, Theo got permission to use the music room after the music teacher's last class. There's only one condition - he has to lock the music room and give the key to the janitor before school closes for the day. Seems like it's not just me who finds him charming.

"Won't you join us, Al?"

I must have zoned out, because suddenly Eliza is sitting in front of the big piano and Theo has his guitar in hand.

"Right, sorry."

Theo and Eliza both start playing, and I sing along. We've really improved, thank god for that at least. The talent show is in a few days, and I want it to turn out good. We practise quite a bit before I realise that I'm going to be late.

"Shit, I've got to go".

"But it's only five o'clock, and we're supposed to be done at six", Eliza says.

"I have a… thing tonight."

"Right, that thing", Theo says.

"What thing?" Eliza asks. "You told him, but not me?"

Eliza sounds hurt. I should have told her as well. I suck. She's still waiting for an answer.

"I'm going to therapy."

Eliza's facial expression changes from upset to even more upset.

"Why wouldn't you tell me that?"

"It's just family therapy, it's not a big deal."

"Not a big deal?" Eliza shouts.

Eliza is getting really angry. She's scaring me a little.

"Okay, girls, let's all take a step back", Theo says.

"No!" Eliza yells at him. I've known you for years, and you talked to him about it and not me? You barely know him!"

I take a few steps back, my eyes filling up with tears. The angry look on Eliza's face changes into a look of sorrow. Before I know it, tears are streaming down my cheeks. Fuck!

"Ally, I'm…"

"Sorry", I say. "I'm so, so sorry."

I turn around and run away crying. As I'm leaving, I can hear Theo yelling at Eliza. He's yelling 'look what you did!' and I can kind of hear Eliza sobbing. I run all the way home, and when I get there mom's standing outside with an angry look on her face.

"You're late."

Right after she says that, she notices that I'm crying. She immediately starts to hug me.

"Oh honey, what happened?"

I can't say or do anything.

"Is this about therapy? If it's this hard for you, we really don't have to go."

"No, it's about…"

I hesitate. I realise I have to tell her.

"It's about Eliza".

"I'm sorry to hear that. Do you still want to go to therapy? We really don't have to today, if it's not a good time."

"No, it's fine. We can go."

"Okay, you go inside and clean up. I'll wait in the car with Annie."

I nod, and then go inside. I wonder what she means by "clean up". When I see myself in the bathroom mirror, I realise what she meant. I have mascara running down from my eyes. I grab a cotton pad with some micellar water on it, and wipe the mascara traces off. Quickly I put some new mascara on, trying not to look completely horrible.

In the car I start thinking about what I'll say to the therapist. I don't want to tell the truth, at least not in front of mom and Annie. We get there pretty quickly. I look at the big building, and I feel sick.

"Are you alright, Alyssa?" Mom asks me.

"I'm fine, just a bit nervous."

We go inside and wait for the therapist. I look around the waiting room. So many people. No one looks happy. That's pretty obvious, but still. My leg starts shaking. I worry. Annie is reading a comic book and mom is looking at her phone. I do nothing. A woman enters the waiting room.

"Tucker", she says.

We rise and follow the woman into a room. The room has a desk, a sofa and a couple of chairs. The woman sits down in one of the chairs and the three of us sit down on the couch.

"Good evening, folks", she says. "And welcome back Alyssa, it's good to see you again."

I recognize the woman now. She's the same therapist that the three of us used to go to.

"Good to see you too."

"Since I haven't seen you in a few months, I want to ask you a few questions. Is that okay?"

She's looking right at me.

"That's okay."

"Wonderful. Why did you stop coming here?"

I look at mom, she's looking at me too. She probably wants to know as well.

"Therapy just felt weird", I say.

The woman nods and writes something down.

"So why are you back now?" she asks.

I look at mom, she's looking down.

"Well, it's not like I have a choice."

"Of course you have a choice, therapy should make you feel better. If it doesn't, it's not necessary to go.

I think about Theo and Eliza. Theo's words echo in my mind. 'I strongly suggest that you get some professional help.' I sigh.

"It's not therapy, it's the whole family therapy thing. I think I would feel better if I went here without my family."

"If that's what would make you feel better, then let's do it."

"No!" Mom protests. "I brought Alyssa here so we can heal together as a family."

"But you go alone, as well. Annie also goes alone. Why can't I go alone?"

The words leave my mouth naturally. I actually talked back to my mom, I can't believe it. The therapist looks at mom.

"It's not that, mom says. "If you want to go alone you can. I just really want you to continue family therapy."

"Why do you want me to go to family therapy so badly?"

"I just want us to heal as a family, the whole family."

"I see where you're coming from, Linda", the therapist says. "But Alyssa is a person with feelings. If she feels that she doesn't want to go, she shouldn't have to."

"I guess you're right", mom sighs.

The therapist continues the session by asking Annie and mom a few questions. I can't be happier when the session finally ends.

"Do you want me to book you for a single session, Alyssa?" The therapist asks me.

"Sure."

During the entire ride home, mom is telling me how proud she is of me for speaking up. When we finally get home, Eliza is sitting at our doorstep. I don't really want to talk to her, but I feel like I have no choice. She is my best friend after all. Mom and Annie go inside while I stay out with Eliza.

"Hey", I say.

"Hey."

Eliza looks sad. I sit down next to her, watching her trying to hold back tears.

"I want to apologise for what I said in the music room. I'm happy for you and Theo, I really am. But I wanted to be the first person you told about therapy."

Her voice is shaking.

"It's okay, I forgive you."

"Really?"

"Yes, you're my best friend and I love you. In fact, I'm sorry for not telling you."

"You don't have to apologise", she says.

I give Eliza a tight hug, and she gently lifts my sleeve. Not so that my scars become visible, but enough to reveal the bracelet. She flips the infinity charm and looks intensively at the engraved text. A drop of water falls on my wrist. Is it raining? No. It's a teardrop from Eliza's eye. The happy look on her face fades into sadness.

"We'll always be friends, right?"

I smile at her.

"Forever."

Eliza smiles back and hugs me. I hug her back. I really don't deserve her.

Chapter 9
Elijah

"Is this correct?" Eliza asks.

"No, that's wrong. Warm air rises, it doesn't sink."

We are sitting in a quiet coffee shop, studying. Eliza needed help, but Theo wasn't available, so I offered to try and help her.

"Damn, since when are you so smart?"

"I study with Theo."

"True…"

Eliza gets quiet, but she's grinning at me.

"Since we ARE on the topic of boys", she finally says, "I can proudly say that I've met someone."

My heart drops. For a brief moment, I feel like a part of me dies. Am I… Jealous? No, I couldn't be. Eliza will always be my best friend, and no boys could ever come between us. Besides, I have a boyfriend too. In fact, I'm happy for Eliza. As I should be.

"Really? That's great", I say in a cheerful tone, not entirely sure I mean it. "Who's the lucky person?"

"That's the best part. It's Elijah!"

My jaw drops to the floor. Elijah? He's literally the cutest guy in school! It makes sense, since Eliza is the cutest girl.

"Wow, that's… unexpected."

It's really not.

"I know!" Eliza squeals. "I have a picture of us, do you want to see it?"

Before I can say anything, Eliza's already taking her phone out from her bag. She hands me the phone, and there it is. A picture of her and Elijah at the beach.

"That's a picture of us on our first date! He took me for a romantic walk on the beach."

I don't respond. I'm too busy studying every bit of the picture. Eliza's beautiful blue curls rest perfectly on

Elijah's chest. She's hugging him sideways, and his arm is wrapped around her waist. Elijah's shirt is so tight, you can see every contour of his upper body. His blonde hair seems so soft, and those blue eyes look like they can cast love spells. Visually, he's perfect in every way. Just what Eliza deserves.

"Yeah, that is romantic", I say after a long pause.

"He didn't serenade me though", she says, grinning.

I can feel my face getting red. Theo really is great.

"Speaking of Theo", Eliza continues. "I was hoping you two would go on a double date with us on Friday."

"Friday? But what about our sleepover?" I ask.

"Relax, we can still sleep over, we'll just go out to dinner with the guys first."

I think about it for a minute.

"Alright, I'll ask Theo."

"Great! Now, does warm air rise or sink?

"Rise, Eliza", I sigh. "Warm air always rises".

On my way home from the coffee shop, I give Theo a quick call.

"Hey, Al! Why are you calling?"

"Eliza invited us to a double date."

"A double date! You need two couples for that, Eliza is as single as they come."

I can feel that burn of jealousy returning, but I try to brush it off.

"Eliza has a boyfriend now."

"Wait, really? She doesn't really seem like the boyfriend type."

"Well, neither am I, so…"

"True. Tell her we'll be there. I can't wait to meet her new boyfriend."

"Neither can I."

We talk for a bit longer and then hang up.

Thursday comes around, and we're practising in the music room.

"I think we're ready for the talent show", Theo says.

"Yes! We will kill it", Eliza squeals.

"Absolutely", says a strange voice from the doorway.

I turn around to see… Elijah?! What's he doing here? He's wearing his signature tight shirt. Eliza starts giggling.

"What are you doing here?" She's smiling excitedly at him.

Eliza's voice changes when she talks to him. It becomes a lot softer, and somewhat high pitched.

"Just checking in on my favourite girl. The janitor told me you'd be here."

"The janitor? You talked to that old scary dude to find me? That's brave."

"I'd like to look brave for my girl."

Elijah seems to bring out the worst in Eliza. He's also super cheesy. I can feel my hands balling into fists.

"And this must be Theo and Ally."

"Pleasure to meet you", Theo calmly replies.

He's holding his hands out for a handshake, but this guy slaps it like a high five.

"You're funny, man. Who does handshakes, right?"

In the corner of my eye, I can see Theo balling his hands into fists, too. I can't imagine us two fighting Elijah. He's so strong, he'd have us both on the ground in seconds.

"Anyways, I better get going, but I'm looking forward to the double date thing tomorrow. Come on babe!"

He puts his arm around Eliza, and they start making their way out. As they walk away, I can see Elijah's hand touching Eliza's butt. It grosses me out.

"Interesting choice, Eliza", Theo says in a dry voice after they've left.

"Really interesting indeed."

"Hey, Al, is there something wrong with my handshakes?"

"Not at all. That guy is just an idiot!"

"I believe you are right."

I'm sitting in Theo's car, feeling nervous. We are on our way to the double date. Both Theo and I are wearing the exact same clothes as we did on our first date. We're going to the same restaurant, too.

"I'm sorry I don't have a gift for you this time", Theo says.

"Oh no, that's fine. Just being on this date is a great gift."

He smiles, still keeping one eye on the road. What he doesn't know is that I've got a gift for him.

We arrive at the restaurant and see Eliza and Elijah standing upfront. Eliza is dressed in a pretty white dress, wearing sparkly light blue jewellery that matches her hair perfectly. She looks really good. Elijah, however, is dressed in a tight t-shirt and shorts. He looks like he's going for a run, rather than on a date.

"Well, well, is that Theo! I could barely recognise you. You're so well dressed", Elijah says.

"I sure recognise you", Theo replies, slightly sarcastically.

They both start laughing, but you can tell things are a bit tense between them.

"Hey, Ally!" Eliza says cheerfully.

"Hey, Elz. I'm so excited for our double date."

I really don't mean that. I already hate Elijah.

Suddenly, Elijah turns to me. Oh no. "I'm really excited, too. Double the trouble! Can I say, Alyssa, you look really good tonight!" He smiles widely.

Is he flirting with me, right in front of Eliza?! Fuck this guy.

"It's weird, because you never look this good in school", he continues.

"Can we not talk about how I look, please?"

I glare at him, using my eyes against him. Showing him what I think about his ways.

"Let's just go inside, okay?" Theo says.

"I can get behind that", Elijah says while shrugging his shoulders. "I'm so hungry, I could eat a horse."

Theo grabs my hand, and we go inside. Elijah and Eliza follow. A nice waitress sits us down at a table and hands us some menus.

"So many options. You've been here before, Ally. What do you recommend?" Eliza asks.

"Definitely the sushi", I reply.

"Oh god no", Elijah whines. "I hate sushi."

Everybody gets quiet.

"I believe Eliza asked Alyssa for her opinion", Theo finally says.

"It's fine, I'll get a salad." Eliza looks unhappy.

"That's more like it", Elijah says. "I'm going to get the steak."

"I hate steak", Theo says.

The boys go into a staring competition. I lean closer to Eliza.

"Listen, get whatever the fuck you want. Don't let that stupid poser tell you what to get", I whisper to her. I'm done with being nice about this whole Elijah deal.

She smiles vaguely at me.

"Okay, I will."

The waitress returns.

"Are you ready to order?"

"I'll have the steak", Elijah says.

"Oh, all right then."

She writes it down, then looks over at Theo.

"I'll have the salmon."

Elijah scoffs. Theo scoffs back. The waitress looks at them back and forth, before finally turning to me.

"I'd like to have the sushi", I say.

"Me too, please", Eliza adds.

Elijah gives her a glare, but she seems to ignore it.

"Alright, I'll make sure that chef gets started with that for you."

The waitress leaves, and I try to start a conversation.

"So, how'd you two meet?" I ask, turning to Eliza and Elijah.

"It's actually a very romantic story", Elijah replies. "So, in Mr Long's class we have assigned seating, and because I kept talking to Brian during class, Mr Long moved me to sit next to Eliza. And as I sat down beside her for the first time, I instantly asked her out."

That's the very romantic story? Please.

"I'm sorry, what's romantic about that?" Theo bluntly asks.

Elijah looks at him, visibly annoyed.

"It's love at first sight!"

"Well, since she was in that class from the beginning, I'm assuming it wasn't really first sight", Theo argues.

"Don't listen to him, babe", Eliza breaks in.

"Don't worry, I won't."

Their faces move closer and closer to each other. Then their lips touch, and they start making out! They're sitting there making out in the middle of the restaurant. I'm getting second hand embarrassment. It's so hard to watch, that I have to bury my face in Theo's upper arm. Theo just watches in pure shock. Once they're finished, Eliza looks embarrassed.

"Excuse me, I'm getting some appetisers from the bar", Theo says while getting up from the chair.

"Right behind you." I rise and follow him up to the bar.

"Do people usually do that on double dates?" Theo asks me, as we're eyeing the snack menu.

"I don't think so."

We order a few appetisers. Theo pays for them, even though I tell him he doesn't have to. When we come back to the table, Eliza is giggling and talking in that high pitched voice again. We sit back down.

"Appetisers! Don't mind if I do", Elijah cheerfully says.

He takes one and swallows it in one bite. Then he takes another one, and feeds Eliza with it. That's something I'd rather not witness again. We manage to finish the plate before our food comes in.

"Alright, let me take this plate to the kitchen", the waitress says.

She picks up the plate, but before she can leave Elijah stops her.

"Excuse me, you messed up my girlfriend's order", he says.

"I'm sorry to hear that, didn't she order the sushi?"

"No, she ordered the Caesar salad."

The waitress looks sceptical. I'm hoping that Eliza is going to stand up for herself. A few seconds go by, and she still says nothing. I look at Elijah. He looks really proud of himself.

"She did order the sushi", I finally say.

"Yeah, I thought so too." The waitress seems stressed and annoyed.

"She ordered sushi because that's what she wanted", I continue. "Right, Elijah?"

Elijah looks angry, but he doesn't say anything. The waitress leaves, and Eliza mumbles a quick 'thank you' in my direction. We eat in silence. The vibe is just too weird for small talk. When we're finished eating, the waitress returns with the bill.

"Are you guys splitting?" she asks.

"Yes, we are", Eliza replies.

"I'll pay for us two", Theo offers, while wrapping his arm around me.

"You really don't have to", I object.

"I want to."

Eliza looks directly at Elijah, expecting him to do the same as Theo.

"I didn't bring any money", Elijah says.

Eliza sighs quietly. "I guess I'll pay for the two of us, then."

"Don't worry about it, I'll pay for all of us", says Theo, trying to save Eliza the embarrassment.

"No, Theo, you don't have to, seriously." Eliza looks like she's about to cry.

"I want to. Besides, it would be rude to have the ladies pay".

He glares at Elijah as he says it, but Elijah seems unbothered.

The waitress nods. "Alright, I'll ring that up for you."

We leave the restaurant. Eliza excuses herself to the lady's room. Theo and I walk to his car, and he helps me get my things out.

"So, that was absolutely terrible", Theo says, looking shook.

"Yeah. It's like you said, Elijah is an interesting choice."

"If we remove him from tonight, I had a great time. I really like you, Alyssa. I want to keep spending time with you."

Theo is so cute. And that reminds me…

"I really like you too. In fact, this time I got you a gift."

I open up my bag and take out the gift. A little box. I hand it to him.

"What is it?"

"Open it, and you'll find out."

He opens the box with fingers that are slightly shaking.

"Wow, Al, that's so pretty. Where'd you get it?"

"I got it at a crystal shop downtown. It's a rose quartz, the lady in the store said it's a love stone."

"I love it. Thank you."

Chapter 10

Eliza

I look at Theo's car, as he drives away from the restaurant. Then I look over at Eliza. Elijah is kissing her. You can really tell from the odd look on Eliza's face, that she doesn't want to be here anymore. Elijah couldn't care less. Once he finally leaves, I walk up to Eliza. She gives me an embarrassed smile.

"Let's go to my place", she suggests.

We walk in silence for a while. Past the supermarket and the train station. We never walk in silence. Not even when there's nothing to talk about. Now that we have so much to talk about, we can't talk. It's almost like we both suddenly went mute.

"Thank you", Eliza suddenly says.

I'm confused. What a strange thing to say.

"Thank you for what?"

"For being so great tonight. The way you stood up for me, I could've never done that for myself."

"Elijah was being a real dick. You deserve better."

"You're right, Ally. I'm going to dump him."

"Sounds good. Can I ask you something, though?"

Eliza nods at me. I hesitate for a bit, but I do really want to know.

"Why would you even go out with him in the first place?"

Eliza looks down.

"I don't really know." She shrugs. "He just asked me out, and I said yes."

She starts giggling.

It's kind of stupid, but... Sometimes I wish you were my boyfriend.

I can feel myself blushing.

"If I was your boyfriend? That would be kind of weird."

"I guess it would be."

Eliza is probably the most important person in my life. I could never even imagine my life without her, that's how important she is. That's how much I love her. I love everything about her. Her smile, her style, and most of all her personality and her heart. I love how well we know each other. She deserves so much more than some disrespectful asshole like Elijah. She deserves someone that can treat her right.

"Ally, are you listening?"

Confused, I look at her. She has her phone in hand. Her face is distressed, staring at the phone screen. I lean over to see what's happening on her device. It's a text from Elijah.

We're done.

"He dumped me!" Eliza looks baffled.

"Well, that's good, right?"

"No, it's not! He shouldn't have the satisfaction of dumping me. Dumping me is something he can brag about to his douchebag friends."

It almost looks like she's going to cry over that bitch boy Elijah.

"Well, let him brag."

Eliza looks up at me.

"I can't. It will be totally humiliating for me!"

"Being dumped is a part of womanhood", I tell her, hearing myself sounding oddly grown up. "If he wants to be the fool who dumped the best girl he ever had, that's his loss."

Eliza smiles slightly.

"Thank you, Ally. You're a good friend."

She gives me a hug, and I hug her back. When we pull away from each other, Eliza's smile is gone.

"What's the matter? Is it Elijah?"

"No, it's…"

Eliza hesitates. She looks around. The streets are empty. She exhales and looks at me.

"…Theo."

Theo? What happened?

"What do you mean? Oh my God, is he being a bitch boy too? Cause if that's the case, I'll break up with him right away!"

"What? No!"

"Okay, now I'm confused. What about Theo, then?"

"Theo is amazing. You're so lucky to have him. I just wish that someday I can have a relationship like yours and Theo's."

"I'm sure you'll find someone soon, Elz."

I wrap my arm around her, and we keep on walking. Theo is a great boyfriend, and Eliza is a great girl. I'm sure she'll find someone like him eventually. The weird, jealous feeling leaves me. It's a big relief. Although I do still wonder why that feeling was there in the first place.

We finally reach Eliza's house and start off with the usual sleepover stuff. Watch movies, talk shit, drink soda and eat snacks. We're having a lot of fun, it's almost like Elijah is completely forgotten. Then suddenly, my phone rings.

"Who is it?" Eliza asks.

I look at my phone.

"It's Theo."

"Well, answer it."

I do as she says. "Hello? Theo?"

"Hey there, Al", Theo says. "I'm just calling to check in on you two after the date."

"What is he saying?" Eliza whispers.

I put my hand over the phone's microphone.

"He wants to check in on us after the date."

"Well, put him on speaker!"

"Hello? Are you there, Al?" Theo says.

I put the call on speaker.

"Yes, we're here, both of us."

"Oh, Eliza too? Perfect."

"I'm here", Eliza confirms.

"I was just shocked by how Elijah acted in that restaurant", Theo says. "He sure is a…"

"Bitch boy?" I suggest.

"…Interesting choice of words, and yes. A total bitch boy."

"It doesn't matter", Eliza sighs. "He dumped me anyway. But like Ally said, his loss."

"HE dumped YOU?!"

Theo blurts it out so loudly that the sound glitches.

"I'm sorry. I just thought that if anything, you would be dumping him."

"That's what I thought too", I agree.

"He was just a bit quicker than me. It's practically mutual." Eliza smiles vaguely.

"It's safe to say that Elijah ruined the evening. I just wanted to make sure you two weren't too bummed out about it. I wouldn't want anything bad to happen."

I'm not entirely sure if he's talking to me or Eliza. He's obviously talking to both of us, but 'I wouldn't want anything bad to happen' sounds like such a 'don't hurt yourself' kind of thing to say.

"It's alright", Eliza says. "We're alright."

"Good. Well, I'll see you two on Monday."

"Great. See you."

"Bye!"

I hang up the phone. Once again, Eliza looks like she's about to cry. We were so happy only a second ago. I thought we were going to ignore all the things that happened earlier.

"Are you alright, Eliza?"

A tear slowly runs down her cheek.

"I'm fine. I just…"

I grab her hand tightly.

"Whatever it is, you can tell me. I love you, and I would never judge you."

Eliza takes a deep breath.

"I've had a lot of friends, and also a few lovers. They all left me. Elijah is just one of them. My own parents don't even have time for me. They work long hours and leave me alone in that cold house. I've known you my whole life, and you're still here, even though I'm not the most loyal friend to you."

Not the most loyal friend? She's always seemed loyal to me. I feel so confused.

"But you are loyal. You've never left me either, throughout all these years. Even though you're prettier and happier than me, we've still managed to stay best friends."

"I've seen the way my other friends look at you, though. And I've never said anything to defend you! I'm such a mean, useless friend."

She starts to cry violently. Poor Eliza, I never realised how much she was suffering being friends with others, while still having me around. Hell, I never realised that she felt like a terrible friend. She's a GREAT friend. It kind of hurts a little bit, knowing that she knew about their dirty looks and never stood up for me, but she's still a great friend. I love her so much.

"Listen, Eliza, you're the best friend I could ever ask for. I love you, and I will continue to love you no matter what."

Eliza smiles slightly and wipes her tears.

"Promise you'll never leave me, Alyssa."

Alyssa? She's never called me Alyssa before. She's called me Ally since we were kids. I smile at her.

"We already promised to be best friends forever, dummy"

"Just give me a hug."

We hug for a long time. I don't ever want to let go of her. Eliza truly is the sun in my life. Shortly after, we go to sleep. I have to wake up early the next morning, to get to my first single therapy session.

The next morning, I get up and start packing my things, so I can leave right after breakfast. I try to pack as quietly as possible, since Eliza is still sleeping. But even though I'm trying my best to be quiet, she wakes up anyway.

"Why are you packing, are you leaving already?" she asks in a sleepy voice.

"I've got a therapy session today. I'm just packing my things so I can leave right after breakfast."

"Oh, alright. Let me help you."

Eliza and I finish packing, and then go downstairs to make pancakes. We usually never make pancakes for breakfast, but we've decided to celebrate the disappearance of Elijah. Not only do pancakes taste good, they're also really fun to make. At least with Eliza. We stack the pancakes on a plate and write: 'fuck the bitch boy!' with jelly on the top pancake. It feels really good to see Eliza smile again. Her smile is so beautiful.

After breakfast, it's time to leave.

"I wish you could stay longer", Eliza sighs.

"So do I."

Eliza gives me a tight hug before I leave for the appointment.

Chapter 11

Therapy

I'm outside the clinic. The large building looks even more intimidating now that I'm here alone. I'm having doubts on whether I should go in or not. I realise I don't have a choice, and finally go inside.

The waiting room looks exactly the same as last time, just less cramped. I guess that not many people go to therapy in the mornings. I approach the receptionist.

"Hi. I have an appointment."

The receptionist looks up from his computer.

"Name?"

"Alyssa Tucker."

He types something on his computer then looks back at me.

"Go to the waiting room on the fourth floor. Doctor Nessa will be right with you."

"Thank you."

The elevator takes me up to the fourth floor. The waiting room there is empty. I'm the only one here. I sit down on one of the couches, and text my mom that I've arrived safely. A few minutes go by, and soon the therapist appears in the doorway. Her smile is friendly and relaxed.

"Hello, Alyssa. Please follow me."

Doctor Nessa walks ahead of me into a therapy room and I go inside. She closes the door behind us.

"Have a seat."

I sit down on a couch. Doctor Nessa picks up a piece of paper and a pen, then sits down in one of the chairs.

"Thank you for coming today, Alyssa. How are you feeling?"

"I'm alright."

She writes something on the paper sheet.

"Is it okay if I ask you some questions?"

"I guess."

Isn't therapy about being asked questions?

"Very well. Tell me, how did it feel when you found out that your father had died?"

I don't really know what I was expecting when she said she wanted to ask questions, but it definitely wasn't this.

"I guess I didn't really believe it. Or, I didn't want to believe it."

I can feel tears burning in my eyes. There's a box of paper tissues on the table in front of me. I grab a few.

"I understand. Have you noticed any changes in your behaviour since then?"

I try to swallow the lump in my throat, but I fail.

"Yes. My grades have dropped, I've started acting cold towards my family, and everything that once seemed important to me doesn't anymore."

Tears stream down my face. I wipe them away with a tissue. Dr Nessa nods at me and takes notes.

"Have you felt like a kind of sadness has been following you wherever you go?"

Holy shit. That's how I feel all the time.

"Yes! I feel like a subtle sadness is just engraved in the back of my mind."

"Don't worry, it's more common than you think. I would really appreciate it if you could tell me more about this sadness."

I take a deep breath.

"It's just always there. Even when I'm happy."

"I see. That's a sign of depression."

My heart drops. I can't be depressed. I'm not depressed. I'm just a little sad.

"Let's explore that feeling some more", Dr Nessa continues.

I nod slightly.

"When do you feel this sadness the most?"

"I don't know. When I'm alone, I guess."

"Do you think about your father when you're alone?"

"Well, yes. I do."

"Can you elaborate your answer? What are you thinking more specifically?"

"Sometimes I wonder if I could have done anything to prevent him from dying. Then I wonder if it's my fault."

Dr Nessa looks at me with big eyes.

"What happened to him was not your fault. Don't blame yourself."

"I know it's not my fault. But when I think of him, I feel like it is."

Tear after tear runs down my face, but I don't sob. I just sit there, crying quietly. I try to dry my tears.

"I want you to know that everything you say in here stays in here, until you decide to tell a family member."

She knows that this goes deeper.

"I'm not going to tell anyone unless you ask me to. Anything you want to tell me, you can."

I debate on whether or not I should tell her. I feel like she already knows.

"This sadness… It's not always there."

Dr Nessa leans forward a little bit. She's making eye contact with me. Her eyes are big.

"It's not there when I cut myself", I continue.

She takes notes. My tears flow like a river.

"Thank you for telling me, Alyssa. You look pretty sad, should we leave it here for today?"

I nod.

"Alright. Do you want to book another session?"

"Yes, please."

After I leave the clinic, the tears stop coming and eventually my face dries up. I try to think about happy things. Like how the talent show is only a week away.

Chapter 12

Small celebration

I'm sitting in the kitchen when the doorbell rings. Who can that be, on a Monday evening? I don't think mom hears the doorbell. She's doing the dishes with her headphones on. Annie is playing upstairs. I figure I have to answer the door, so I get up and do it. I expect it to be a package delivery, but when I open the door, I'm greeted by Theo and Eliza.

"Surprise!" they yell.

Theo has his laptop in hand, and Eliza is holding a plastic bag. I laugh.

"What are you two doing here?"

"We thought we'd surprise you with a movie night!" Eliza squeals.

"Yeah, you know, to celebrate the talent show", Theo says.

"Celebrate already? It hasn't even started yet."

"True, but I already know that we're going to win. No one has practised more than us", Theo assures me.

"Don't say that."

"Are you going to let us in, or what?" Eliza says, before letting herself in.

Theo follows and they march upstairs. I close the front door. They're so silly, I'm so happy to have them! When I go into my room, Theo is already setting up his laptop and Eliza is unpacking the plastic bag, which happens to be full of snacks. I open my wardrobe and take out my favourite sweatpants and an oversized shirt, and then change into them quickly. I undo my bra underneath the shirt and throw it into the closet. When I turn around, both Theo and Eliza are looking at me, smiling weirdly. I can feel my face turning red. I kind of forgot that they were there for a moment, I just wanted some cosy clothes for the movie night.

Eliza is sitting on my bed, and Theo is standing next to her. I sit down with Eliza. My bed is rather big, but it's definitely not made for three people to sit on it. I have to move really close to Eliza in order to leave room for Theo. He finally sits down next to me. I'm pretty much cramped in between the two of them. Glad I'm not claustrophobic.

"Which movie do you guys want to watch?" Theo asks us.

"Anything but a romcom", Eliza says. "A thriller or an adventure."

"As interesting as that sounds, romcoms are still superior", Theo replies.

"Well, then Ally gets to decide. What do you want to watch?"

I smile. I know exactly what I want to watch.

"A horror movie."

"No, no, no!" Eliza whimpers. Remember when you made me watch that one horror movie when we were little, and I peed myself!?"

Theo starts laughing.

"Sounds like a great memory", he says in between laughs.

"Oh, it was great", I agree, laughing with him.

Eliza's face turns red from embarrassment.

"Fine! We'll watch a horror movie. Just not anything too scary."

Theo hands me the computer so I can pick out a movie. I find one I want to watch.

"How about this one?"

"That looks alright", says Theo.

"It looks a bit scary." Eliza sounds sceptical.

"That's kind of the point", I tell her. "Besides, it's a thirteen plus, you'll be fine."

Eliza looks hesitant, but finally gives in.

"Turn it on", she sighs.

I press play and put down the computer on my desk. It's a good movie, not the best I've seen, but okay. I look over at Theo. He looks kind of scared but plays it off cool. My eyes meet his, and we lock eyes for a moment.

I can sort of see him smiling at me in the dark. He grabs my hand. Suddenly, I feel a grip around my other arm. I look down and see Eliza's hands wrapped tightly around it. There's a jump scare. Eliza flinches, whimpers and buries her face in my shoulder. I giggle slightly. I feel a little bad for her, but she's really cute when she's scared.

"I think that's enough scary movies for Miss Goldberg tonight", I say.

I pause the movie and Eliza looks up from my shoulder. "Oh, thank god."

Suddenly there's a knock on my bedroom door.

"Come in", I say.

Mom walks in with an annoyed look on her face.

"Alyssa Tucker, I never said that you could have friends over!"

Oh no, she's using my full name.

"We're sorry, Mrs Tucker", Theo says regretfully. "We were the ones who showed up here uninvited."

"Yeah, we're sorry", says Eliza. "We just wanted to come here to celebrate that we entered the upcoming talent show."

Mom looks at them back and forth. She sighs.

"I want you two out of here by ten."

"Thanks, mom!" I feel relieved.

Mom nods at me and leaves the room, closing the door behind her. Theo looks at us with a weird face.

"If we're not going to watch the movie, then what are we doing?"

I look at my makeup bag, then at Eliza. She's also looking at the makeup bag, then at me. We give each other a slightly evil look, then we look at Theo. His facial expression changes from confused to scared.

"He has really good cheekbones", Eliza points out.

"And big, non-hooded eyes", I add.

"What are you guys talking about?"

I lift up Theo's chin slightly. I get a good look at all his features. They're kind of perfect.

"Get the bag, Elz. Get the fucking bag."

"Happy to oblige."

Eliza reaches for the makeup bag.

"How should we do this?" she asks me.

I grab my kohl eyeliner from the bag and draw a line down the middle of Theo's face.

"Are you up for a challenge? You do one side of the face and I'll do the other. Theo will be the judge."

"Hell yeah! Let's do it."

"Can I just ask a teeny-tiny question?" Theo asks in a dry voice. "What are you going to do to my face?"

"We're going to make it even more beautiful with makeup!" Eliza exclaims.

"Not that you need it, though", I add, smiling sweetly at Theo.

Then, his whole mood suddenly changes.

"No! I don't want to. Stop it."

"Come on, it will be fun", Eliza says. "A little makeup never hurt anybody."

Theo's eyes fill with tears.

"What's wrong?" Eliza asks him.

"Perhaps it's best if we just drop it, Eliza." I'm starting to feel uncomfortable, looking at Theo's pained face expression.

"I just don't want to look like a girl", he says. His voice sounds muffled, and he looks so sad.

"You don't look like a girl", I protest. "I'm sorry if this whole makeup thing made you feel bad."

I put my hand on his shoulder. He tries to dry off the tears with his sleeve.

"Ally's right, Eliza says. You don't look like a girl. Can I ask why you don't want to look like one? It's just for fun, you know."

Theo looks like he's trying to swallow a huge lump in his throat.

"I'm transgender, female to male", he says quietly.

"Oh my god, I'm so sorry. I didn't know." Eliza sounds panicky.

"I'm sorry too. I knew about it, and I still tried to put makeup on you. I really suck."

"You don't suck! I accept your apologies." Theo smiles vaguely.

Eliza nods at him, also smiling.

"We should go home, it's almost ten anyway", Theo says.

"Yeah, it is. Thanks for visiting, guys."

Theo and Eliza gather their things and leave. After they've gone, I start laughing to myself. Theo left without washing off the line I drew across his face. I'm a bit worried about him though, so I send him a text. He assures me that it's fine, and tells me that it felt good telling Eliza. I hope he really means it.

Chapter 13

Showtime

The last couple of days have been stressful. Theo, Eliza and I have been practising like crazy for the talent show. The day is finally here. Eliza and I are doing makeup in the school restroom. Neither one of us have seen Theo yet, he's off setting everything up in the auditorium.

"What do you think, Ally?"

I look at Eliza. She looks stunning. She's got a bold eyeshadow look going on. The makeup matches her black rhinestone dress perfectly. I find myself mesmerised by her beauty.

"You're beautiful, like a work of art."

"Thank you, I think your makeup looks great too."

"Really? Thank you."

Eliza smiles at me, but the look in her eyes tells me that something is wrong.

"Are you alright, Elz?"

Her facial expression doesn't change at all.

"Yeah… I'm just kind of nervous."

"I am too."

Eliza lifts up one of the sleeves on my dress slightly. She looks at the bracelet and turns over the infinity charm. I look at the bracelet, and the engraved text.

"You'll always be my Ally", she says softly.

I look up from the bracelet and Eliza is looking back at me with tears in her eyes. She takes my hand, and hugs me with her other arm. I stay silent, and hug her back. I have to stand on my toes to be able to rest my chin on her shoulder. She pulls away from me.

"I'm sorry, Ally. I'm just so proud of you."

"Proud of me?" I laugh. "Why?"

"You got help for your problem. Your grades are better."

"Now you sound like my mom."

"I'm proud of you for being a good friend, a great girlfriend and just a fantastic person in general. I love you, Ally, and I never want you to change."

"I couldn't have done it without you, Elz. I love you too."

We just stand there for a few seconds looking at each other. All of a sudden Eliza grabs my hand.

"Come on, we don't want to miss the talent show", she says with a mischievous smile.

We leave the main building and walk over to the auditorium. The talent show hasn't started yet, we're still early. Walking through the double doors, we see a bunch of students and teachers setting up equipment for the show. It's easy to spot Theo in the crowd. He's wearing all black and a pair of silly sunglasses. He comes sprinting towards us with a huge smile as soon as he sees us.

"Perfect, you're here!" he exclaims.

"We are", Eliza confirms. "I like your outfit."

"Yeah, I like your sunglasses", I add, giggling.

Theo starts laughing.

"Thanks bullies, I like your outfits too. Now, here's how it goes down - we're the first act, and after we're done we'll have a seat over there."

Theo points to a couple of seats not too far away from where we're standing. A keyboard and a guitar has been set up for us on stage. His words echo in my head. 'We're the first act'. An unsettling nervous feeling is spreading inside of me. A lump in my throat forms, I try to swallow it but I can't. Theo gets a hold of my hand.

"I can see you're slightly freaked out. That's alright. You'll have both me and Eliza right next to you the whole time."

I look at Eliza. She nods at me. I feel my courage returning.

"Okay then, let's do this."

We go sit down in our seats while we wait for the show to start. Other students start coming in. Soon enough the room is filled with the sound of chatter. I look around. Most of the students have their normal clothes on, but some of them are wearing obvious stage costumes. You can clearly see what their talents are, just by looking at the costumes. There's even a guy in a top hat and a cape - of course there's bound to be a magician. To be honest, I'm not as sure as Theo that we will win this thing.

Suddenly there's a tap on one of the microphones. It's the vice principal. She clears her throat and the room goes quiet.

"Welcome, students, to the very first school talent show!" She says in a loud and cheerful voice.

The students start applauding, and the vice principal has to quiet them down.

"We will soon start with our first talents, but before that I would like to thank everyone who helped me organise this show."

The students start to cheer again. I cheer too. I cheer for Eliza.

"Alright then, let's begin. Our first talent act is a nameless band that consists of three students."

The three of us stand up as the vice principal keeps introducing our band. We step on to the stage. I never really thought about us as a band, but it feels right.

"Showtime", Theo whispers to us.

Eliza gets behind the keyboard and Theo picks up the guitar. This is it. The vice principal stops talking and hands me the microphone. All the nervous feelings leave my body as soon as Theo and Eliza begin playing. It's like the auditorium is empty. There's only the three of us. I start singing. Theo sings with me, even though he doesn't have a microphone. I'm the only one they can hear. I love the sound of us. We are nailing it!

The song ends after about two minutes. After a moment of silence, the cheering and applauding starts.

Most of it is probably for Eliza, but I'd like to think that they cheer for me and Theo as well.

"Thank you so much!" Theo shouts.

The vice principal comes back out on stage. I hand her the microphone and get off the stage with Theo and Eliza.

"Alright, that was Alyssa Tucker, Theodore Andersson and Eliza Goldberg with Battery Is Running Low. Now we have a group of glamorous boy band lovers…"

The vice principal's voice fades out as the three of us are talking.

"That went so well!" I say, excited.

"I know", Theo says. "I'm so proud of both of you."

"We were SO good", Eliza concludes.

"Yeah, you guys were really good", a sudden voice says.

It's a cute girl, sitting in the row behind us. She has straight black hair and dark brown eyes. She's wearing simple makeup and normal clothes, so I figure she isn't a contestant.

"Thank you", says Theo.

"Yeah thank you, what's your talent?" Eliza asks her.

"Oh, I'm just here to watch. I'm Yuki, by the way."

"Nice to meet you", I say.

"Yeah, nice to meet you", Eliza says. "You look so cute, I thought you were a contestant for sure."

Yuki looks at Eliza, almost as if in disbelief.

"Wow, thank you! That means a lot coming from someone like you."

Before Eliza can respond, the music starts and we all turn our heads to the stage. The entire show lasts for about two hours. There are a lot of contestants. Singing, dancing, magic, and a couple of really unusual talents. It's super entertaining. So many different people doing so many different things.

"Alright, that was our last talent", the vice principal finally announces. "Now me and the principal are going to decide the winner. "

Whispers and laughter fill the room. Everyone is wondering who will win. With so many great acts, it's anybody's guess.

"Hey, where do you guys want to go after this?" Theo asks us.

"Perhaps we should go get ice cream to celebrate our great performance!" Eliza suggests.

I instantly agree. "Ice cream sounds great."

The principal and vice principal enter the stage, and the room goes quiet with suspense. The principal takes the microphone.

"Before I reveal the winner, I would like to thank all of the contestants and let you know that this was not an easy choice."

"Blah blah blah, just tell us who the winner is", Eliza whispers.

"And now, to the winner. The winner of THE FIRST EVER talent show is…"

The wait is literally killing all of us.

"Battery is running low! Congratulations, guys!"

What, we won?! Holy shit! Everybody is applauding and cheering for us. I can't believe it!

"Alyssa Tucker, Theo Andersson, Eliza Goldberg, get up here!"

My hands cover my mouth. I'm so shocked. I look at Theo and Eliza. Eliza seems to have the same reaction as me, while Theo's just smiling like a crazy person.

"You heard the man, come on!"

Theo grabs my hand and practically drags me with him. Eliza follows. On stage, the principal hands us each a diploma, and the vice principal gives us one red rose each. Theo gets a hold of the microphone. Me and Eliza exchange looks. What now?

"Dear fellow students", he begins. "I'm not blind, and I'm not stupid either. I know that some of you think that I'm weird, and that's okay. I'm new to this school, so it's expected.

He turns to me and Eliza.

"Alyssa and Eliza, you two saw past my weirdness, and for that I thank you. I hope we can continue making music together."

He smiles at us. I smile back at him. His sunglasses actually look cool on stage. The vice principal hands me another microphone. I hold it between Eliza and I.

"We couldn't have done it without Theo, I say, looking straight at him. "This is your song, Theo, and we are just thankful for getting to perform it with you."

"Thank you for everything," Eliza says, also looking at Theo.

The audience cheer for us once more. I hand the microphone back to the vice principal.

"Thank you for listening!" Theo says, before returning the microphone to the principal.

We leave the auditorium shortly after. Lots of people come up to congratulate us. I'm surprised at how many people tell me I am good at singing. Maybe I am talented, after all. We try to find Yuki, the nice girl who sat behind us, to invite her for ice cream with us. But we can't find her anywhere. It's like she's disappeared.

"I guess it's just us, then", Theo says. "Same old gang."

"A fun old gang", Eliza says, giggling.

"For sure!"

We go get ice cream, then part ways to go home. As soon as I get home, I tell mom and Annie that we won. Mom gets super excited.

"That's so great, honey!"

"It is. But I'm going to bed now, I'm tired."

I fall asleep almost immediately. What a day!

Chapter 14

Relationships

I wake up to the sound of raindrops on my bedroom window. God, I love rain! It's so calming, for some reason. Then I realise, the raindrops are the only thing I can hear. No coffee maker, no noise from Annie's room. I sit up and grab my phone. There's a message from mom.

"I had a work emergency. I didn't want to wake you up, so I sent Annie to a friend's house. - Love, mom."

Good, so nothing bad has happened. She sent the message at ten. How long have I been asleep? I realise it's twelve o'clock already. Jesus Christ! I don't know when I last slept in this much.

I get out of bed and go downstairs to make myself something to eat. The house is quiet. I search the freezer for a microwavable meal. I start heating one up and wait. Outside the window the rain is pouring, the wind is blowing through the trees, and Theo… Theo?!

What is Theo doing outside my house in the rain?

He's looking around like a confused sheep. I can't just stand by and watch him get soaked in the rain. I rush to open the front door.

"Theo!" I shout through the pounding sound raindrops on the roof.

He sees me and starts running towards me.

"We need to talk", he says.

I sigh.

"You and Eliza really have to stop coming here uninvited. Anyway, mom is not home, so…"

"Can I come in or not?"

I move out of his way and he comes inside, closing the door behind him. He takes off his soaked jacket and we go to sit down in the kitchen.

"What do we need to talk about?"

"Well… I've been thinking. I like you so much, Alyssa, but I'm not sure that I like you… you know, like that. In fact, I like who I am with you."

I nod. I think I understand what he's saying.

"So you're breaking up with me?"

"Well, yes. But I still really like us to be friends, is that okay?"

"Of course. I want to be friends with you, always."

"So, you're not mad?"

"No, I'm not. I think it's really brave of you to come here and break up face to face. Most guys wouldn't do that."

"Thanks, Ally. That means a lot."

Theo stays for a bit, and we talk. He eventually has to leave. For some reason I don't want to be left alone. I remember the food in the microwave. I take it out, and surprisingly It's still warm. While eating it, I think about Theo's words. 'I like who I am with you'. Seems about right. I don't think I ever liked Theo "like that", either. He's just a very good friend.

After finishing lunch, I go upstairs to get ready for the day. I don't know what I'm getting ready for. I don't have any plans. I go downstairs again and watch TV. I hate being home alone. The presence of mom and Annie is comforting, but I never realised that until now, that they're both out of the house.

Suddenly, there's another knock on the door. What is it now?

I get up from the couch and open the door. It's Eliza. She's holding a big bag.

"You've got to stop coming here uninv…"

She interrupts me by pulling me into a hug. Her tight grip feels unsettling. Something is up. I only notice the look of sorrow in her eyes, once she pulls away.

"I'm sorry for just barging in like this", she says.

I don't say anything. I can tell she needs me right now.

"I kind of need a place to stay for the night."

Her voice is breaking. She's trying really hard not to cry.

"Yes, of course. Come inside."

Eliza smiles at me. We go upstairs to my room, and she puts her bag down.

"Sorry I didn't call before I came. Dad took my phone."

"It's alright. Can I ask why you can't stay at your own house, though?"

The look of sorrow in her eyes returns.

"I don't really want to talk about it. Where's Annie and your mom?"

"Mom had a work emergency, and Annie is at a friend's house."

"Okay."

The vibe is awkward. I have to think of something to say.

"Is this a bad time to tell you that Theo broke up with me?"

Eliza's pupils expand and she lets out a gasp. "He did WHAT?!"

"Keep your voice down. I have neighbours, you know."

"Right, sorry."

The fire in Eliza's eyes is back, and she seems weirdly energised by the news.

"How'd he break up with you?"

"He came over and told me."

"So, you and Theo aren't together anymore?"

She almost seems happy.

"No."

"And you're okay with that?"

"Yes, I think it was for the best. We're not into each other, you know, like that."

"You know what we should do?" Eliza asks.

"What?"

"It's Saturday and we're both single. We should totally go to a party!"

A party? I've never been to a party outside of Eliza's birthday parties.

"I don't know. Where would we even find a party to go to?"

"My friend's cousin is throwing a party on the other side of town. Please, can we go?"

"But I have nothing to wear", I argue.

"Then let's go shopping!"

I think for a bit. I've never been to a party before, and I do like shopping.

"Mom would never let me go."

Suddenly, we hear the sound of the front door opening downstairs.

"We're home!" mom shouts.

"Then let's lie to her", Eliza whispers.

Before I can say anything, Eliza takes my hand and runs downstairs. Mom looks kind of shocked to see Eliza.

"Hi, Eliza. I didn't know you were coming over."

"Eliza's here!" Annie exclaims, overjoyed.

She gives Eliza a hug.

"I was actually wondering if I could sleep over here tonight", Eliza says.

"Well, you didn't sleep over last night, and it is the weekend. I don't see why not, mom replies.

"Thank you, Mrs Tucker. Ally and I were actually planning to go to the mall today."

"That sounds like fun."

I'm suddenly thinking 'fuck it, let's do this.'

"Yeah, and tonight we would like to go to Theo's house", I hear myself lying.

"Sounds like you have a plan", mom says.

"Let's go upstairs and get ready for the mall now", Eliza says, slightly pulling my arm.

"I'm coming."

We rush upstairs and into my room.

"Sick lie", Eliza whispers.

"Shut up."

I get my purse, we do a mirror check, and then we're off.

"Bye, mom!"

Mom comes running into the hallway as we're about to leave. She's got money in her hand.

"Wait. Take this. Buy yourself something nice, okay?"

I look at the money in disbelief as she hands it over to me. It's a good amount. Mom has never given me this much money, at least not so randomly. I look up at her. Her face is blank.

"Thank you, I will."

Mom nods at me.

Eliza and I leave for the mall. When we get there, it's packed. So many people. I suddenly feel very anxious. I feel like everyone is watching me, judging me. It feels good though, to have Eliza beside me. She's the stereotypical pretty girl with her beautiful blue curls and tall, slender silhouette, that everyone admires. Her presence somehow makes me feel pretty, too. Like I'm good enough to hang out with her. The more I look at her, the faster my heart beats. I have a hard time looking away.

"Ally, hello?" Eliza's voice suddenly pierces through my thoughts.

"Yes?"

Has she been talking to me this whole time?

"Look at these dresses, aren't they cute?"

I look at the two dresses she's holding up. They're absolutely gorgeous! They're matching too. Same model but different colours - one black, one white.

"Woah, I like!"

"I know, right!? Should we try them on?"

It's not even a question.

"Yes!"

We find the changing rooms and get into the same booth, since there's only one available.

"Which dress do you want to try on?" Eliza asks me.

"I think the white one would really suit your features, so I'll try on the black."

"Great! Knock yourself out."

We start changing. Once I have the black dress on, I look in the mirror. I really do look pretty in it. This is the most confident I've felt in a long time.

"Wow, Ally."

Eliza looks at me with a sad smile. Our eyes meet in the mirror. What's up with her?

"You look so pretty", she tells me.

My heart starts beating faster and my face gets hot.

"You look really pretty too", I say. I really mean it. She's rocking the white dress.

Eliza giggles. "Thank you. So we're buying these, then?"

"Yes! I mean, if you want to get them."

"I do."

We change clothes and go to pay for our new dresses. I look at the money in my purse. I still have so much left.

"What are you going to do with all that money?" Eliza asks.

I look around where I'm standing. Something specific is catching my eye.

"I know just the thing. I only need mom to approve first."

Eliza notices what I'm looking at.

"Great choice. Call her right away."

I give mom a call, and she gives me the go ahead. Eliza and I start walking towards our goal - the hair salon.

Luckily, the ladies at the salon are able to fit me in straight away. I know exactly what kind of hairstyle I want. Eliza and I talk, while the hairdresser works. When she shows me the finished look, I can't believe my eyes. It's so much better than I expected. My hair is now cut down to my shoulders and I've got bangs.

"What do you think?" The hairdresser asks me.

"It's perfect! Thank you so much."

I pay for the haircut. Eliza hasn't said a thing since the hairdresser showed us the finished result. The look in her eyes is the same, but just a lot more intense. As we walk out of the mall, she remains quiet. I'm starting to worry.

"Hey, Eliza. What's up with you?"

"What do you mean?"

"The way you look at me, your sad smiles, what's up with that?"

Eliza looks down at the ground.

"Oh, that. I don't know what to tell you. You're just so beautiful and smart. You're perfect."

Did Eliza just tell me that I'm perfect? She's literally the definition of perfect.

"If I'm perfect, then you're a goddess", I laugh. "You're the best person I know."

"Really?"

"Yes, really!"

"I like you a lot, Ally. You're my favourite person."

"You're my favourite person too, Elz."

We share a hug, then make our way back home. I look at Eliza's hand. I slightly reach out as if to grab it, but then change my mind. I want to brush my fingers against hers so bad, but I hold back. I'll do it.. Some day. I watch her curls flow in the wind. It makes me realise something. Something I would rather not have realised.

I love her.

I'm in love with Eliza.

Chapter 15

Party

"Here we are!" Eliza exclaims cheerfully.

We get off the bus. I look around the neighbourhood. The houses are big and expensive looking. Still I can't hear any music that could potentially come from a party. I look over at Eliza. There's a certain spark in her blue eyes. She must be really thrilled to go to this party.

"Excited, huh?"

"Yes! I'm SO excited, because you're here with me."

I let out a slight giggle. She's really won me over this time. I could never see myself going to a party without her.

"Let's go look find your party", I say.

Eliza laughs.

"Find it? I know this neighbourhood like the back of my hand. Come on, I'll show you where it is."

Before I can say anything, she takes my hand. All words escape me at that moment. It's weird, because I'm used to holding Eliza's hand all the time. We would hold hands when we were little, and we sometimes hold hands even now as teenagers. But after realising that I'm in love with her, I'm suddenly nervous when it comes to hand holding. I look at her slim fingers in between mine.

We start walking, and she's still holding my hand.

That's when it hits me.

If I'm in love with Eliza, does that make me a lesbian? I don't ever think that I've loved someone, like I love Eliza. I've never really been interested in boys either. I did however date Theo for a little while. Sexuality seems a very confusing thing.

"Look, Ally, there it is!"

I look up. There's a massive house in front of us, with loud music playing from somewhere inside. The street is full of randomly parked cars.

"Let's go inside", Eliza says.

"Shouldn't we knock first?"

"Knock? This is a party, let's just enter!"

That's kind of odd. I figure that I shouldn't question it, though, unused to parties as I am. We walk in.

"Woah", I blurt out.

We're greeted by neon lights and a bunch of people dancing to the loud music, right there in the hallway. I just stand there, shocked.

"Pretty cool, right?" Eliza says. "Come on, let's dance."

Eliza drags me to the dance floor, which is pretty much the entire downstairs of the house. Her white dress shines so beautifully in the neon lights. She lets go of me and starts dancing. She puts her hands in the air and shakes her body to the rhythm of the music. A lot of the boys are looking at her in sheer admiration. Some of the girls too.

"Come on, Ally. Dance with me!"

I smile and giggle. How could I say no to Eliza, with her loving eyes looking at me like that? I try to dance like her, but it's hard to keep up. She's a really good dancer. She sees me struggling and reaches out her hand, drags me along in her dance. There's nothing else at this moment. Just me, the music and Eliza. It kind of feels like we're levitating.

I look at Eliza the whole time. The wide, happy smile, and the flow of her curls along her back and shoulders.

That's when I realise how dangerously close our lips are to each other. I close my eyes, getting ready to kiss her.

"All that dancing is making me tired", she suddenly says.

Oh. So we weren't about to kiss.

"Yeah, me too", I agree, trying not to sound disappointed.

"Let's find a place to sit down."

We're able to find a free couch. I assume it's still empty because it's so small. Most of the party people hang out in cliques. We sit down, close to each other. I look at Eliza's face, only inches away from mine.

"Do you usually go to these kinds of parties?"

"I try to go to them once in a while to keep up with my friends. They're quite fun, but every time I'm there I think, 'I wish Ally was here with me.'"

I hit her lightly on the arm.

"No you don't, stop lying."

"I'm not!"

"Yes, you are."

Eliza hits me back.

"Well, even if I was, I'd still be right. This is more fun with you."

"I wouldn't be here if it wasn't for you."

She looks at me, visibly confused.

"Is that a good or a bad thing?"

"Yo, Eliza", a masculine voice says behind us.

I turn around and see a bunch of people. Both guys and girls. A boy with black hair is standing in front of them all. I assume that's the guy who was talking. I recognise some of these people from school, but most of them I've never seen before.

"Hey guys, what are you doing here?" Eliza says in a cheerful voice.

"Same as you, here for the party", says the guy with the black hair. "Care to join us?"

Eliza looks at me.

"Go, have fun. I'll be okay", I assure her.

She looks at me with an "are you sure" kind of look. I nod at her.

"Alright, I guess I could hang with you guys for just a bit."

"Sweet!"

Eliza walks off with them. Fuck, why did I let her go? Now I'm all alone at this stupid party! I can feel the anxiety growing. I need to find something to help me ignore it. I take a stroll around the house and search for something fun to do, but nothing really catches my attention. I feel thirsty, so I go to find the kitchen.

The kitchen is really big, and empty. There's an island in the middle with snacks and fruit punch. I grab a plastic cup and fill it with the punch, then reach for the snacks. So many options! I don't know which one to choose. I hear another person coming into the kitchen followed by a familiar humming. Wait, what…? I suddenly feel a tap on my shoulder.

"Excuse me… Do you know if there's any alcohol in this?"

The voice sounds very familiar. It couldn't be…! I turn around to see…

"Theo?!"

"Alyssa?! What are you doing here?"

"What are you doing here?"

"The host thought that my talent show performance was fantastic and invited me. Now you go."

"I'm here with Eliza."

"Does your mom know that you're here?"

"Does your mom know that you're here?"

"Of course she does. I could never lie to my mother."

I sigh.

"Of course you couldn't."

"Exactly."

"So, should we go our separate ways and pretend this never happened?"

"No, not happening."

I sigh again.

"What do you want, Theo?"

"What do you mean?"

"I mean, what do I need to give you that will make you leave me alone tonight?"

I feel kind of done with him at this point. Theo stands there, thinking for a second.

"Take me back."

"What? No!"

"Why not, Al?"

"First of all, you broke up with me."

"I know, and it was probably the biggest mistake I've ever made."

I look at Theo. Even though the lights in the kitchen are bright, his pupils look huge. The more I look at him, the more certain I get. He's under the influence of alcohol, or drugs, or both. I should've known. A guy as vulnerable as him is easy to drug and laugh at. But I'm not going to tell him that.

"Go home, Theo."

"What?"

"Go home. This is not a safe environment for someone like you."

His eyes fill with confusion, then anger.

"Are you saying that just because you want me gone?"

I can't believe him! Here I am trying to save him from humiliation, or worse, and he thinks I just don't want him around?

"Please, just go home."

"No!"

I slam my drink on the kitchen island and get a hold of his shoulders.

"Listen, these kids are going to eat you alive! As your friend, I'm telling you to go home and keep yourself safe."

The look in Theo's eyes suddenly changes. They change in… realisation?

"What have they been giving you? Drugs? Alcohol?"

"I… smoked."

"Then you'd better leave quickly. Go home and sober up."

He nods at me.

"Thank you, Ally. I'm sorry."

With that, Theo leaves the kitchen. I hope he leaves the party as well. I sigh deeply and taste my drink. It tastes cheap.

I go back to the party, trying to pretend that nothing just happened. I should probably look for Eliza. She could be anywhere. This house is huge.

I can't find her downstairs. I go upstairs, and there I'm greeted by a bunch of boys. Teenage boys make me nervous. I turn around to walk back downstairs, when I suddenly feel a hard slap on my butt. The sound of the slap is really loud and it hurts, I hate it. I immediately turn my head, and see the face of the person who slapped me. I don't know whether to be shocked or grossed out, when I see it's Elijah. He looks at me like in aw. Then, a wide smirk spreads across his face.

"Alyssa, I didn't recognise you. You look a lot better in the dark."

Is he really calling me ugly, after literally having no problem flirting with me in front of Eliza? I look at the drink in my hand and without thinking, I throw it right at his face. His friends gasp behind him.

"I gave you a compliment, and this is the thanks I get?" he yells, while trying to wipe his face dry using his awfully tight shirt.

"You literally sexually harassed me. You should be glad that you only got a drink thrown in your ugly face!"

"I didn't harass anyone!"

I roll my eyes.

"Slapping butt is a compliment!"

I throw the empty cup on the floor. I look him dead in the eye. Then I realise, I have absolutely nothing more to say. Him and his bitch boy friends are waiting for me to say something, and I'm out of words. I look around. My eyes stop at Elijah's crotch, then move down to my own foot. I hesitate. Elijah and his friends start laughing at me. Saying I look flustered.

"Fuck it", I mumble to myself.

I kick and slam my foot into Elijah's crotch as hard as I can. He instantly falls to his knees, hands covering his genitals and squeaking with pain. Finally, it's my turn to smirk. Watching this person down on his knees, soaked in fruit punch. His friends stand there in shock, staring down at him.

"What the fuck?" one of them blurts out at me.

"Yeah, seriously", says another one. "That's the one place where you can't kick a man."

Elijah's friends all start calling me psycho and asking what's wrong with me. Elijah himself is still on his knees, making noises. I flip all of them off before walking away. Pretty soon after that, I finally find Eliza. She's talking to Yuki, the girl from the talent show. I walk over to them.

"Eliza, you won't believe what just happened!"

"Theo called me", Eliza says.

"What? What did he want?"

"He said something about you telling him to go home. I didn't even know he was here."

"He was stoned, I was worried about him."

Eliza nods. "I see."

"What's the thing that happened?" Yuki asks.

I smirk.

"Eliza's ex, Elijah, slapped me on the butt."

"Oh my god, are you okay, Ally?" Eliza asks in a worried voice.

"Yeah, he's not, though."

Yuki and Eliza look at each other. Yuki has a troubled look on her face.

"What do you mean?"

"I kicked him in the nuts", I giggle.

Eliza's stares at me with big eyes, and then she starts laughing.

"It's great, isn't it?" I can't stop smiling about the whole thing.

"Yes, yes, yes! Karma!"

We laugh like crazy, we cannot seem to stop. When we finally look over at Yuki, she seems a little uncomfortable.

"Where is he now?" she asks, still worried looking.

"Last time I saw him he was on his knees in pain. Why?"

"Well, then you need to get out of here before he gets back on his feet."

Surprised, we're trying to understand what Yuki is saying.

"You guys took the bus, didn't you?"

We nod simultaneously.

"Come with me", Yuki says with a sigh.

She takes out a set of car keys from her bag and starts walking towards the main entry. We follow her out. In the street, we get into Yuki's car, and I give her the directions to my house.

"Is this it?" She eventually asks, braking in front of my house.

"Yeah, this is me. Thanks for the ride, Yuki."

"My pleasure. And don't toy with the bitch boys of the school again, it won't be a good experience."

Eliza and I step out of the car and go inside. Mom is up.

"It's late", she says.

"I know, and I'm sorry."

Her eyes switch focus to Eliza.

"It's fine, I'll let it slide just for tonight."

"Thanks, mom."

"Eliza, I got a call from your dad."

Eliza instantly looks worried.

"He said he wants you home, and that he wants to apologise."

Apologise? I think I might be missing something here.

"Okay. I'll go get my bag", Eliza says.

She kneels down to take off her shoes.

"That's okay", I quickly say. "I'll get it for you."

I hurry up the stairs to get her bag. I can't help but reacting to the dull tone of her voice. Something about the whole thing feels unsettling. I go back downstairs and hand her the bag.

"Thanks, Ally. I should get going."

"Are you going to be alright?" I ask her.

She gives me a nod and warm smile. I hug her tightly before she leaves. She closes the door behind her. I turn to mom, who is staring at me with intense eyes.

"Come on, let's talk in the kitchen."

Chapter 16

Anonymous_storksville

I follow mom into the kitchen. She points to a chair.

"Have a seat."

I sit, and she sits down across the table.

"I know everything."

My heart drops. What does she mean by that? I could be anything. Did my therapist lie to me? Did she tell my mom about the cutting? I have to stay calm.

"What do you mean?"

"I know that you weren't at Theo's house."

I feel relieved since this isn't about my well being, but I'm not exactly thrilled about mom knowing that I lied to her either.

"How did you know that?"

"Well, I called Theo's mother and she said that you and Eliza weren't there. She also told me that he was at a party on the other side of town."

"What does him being at a party have to do with this?"

"I saw that you bought a bus ticket to a station very close to the same party Theo was at."

I realise that she knows the full story.

"Okay, okay! I'm sorry. I won't do it again."

Mom sighs.

"I'm not mad that you went to a party. You're only sixteen once in your life, I want you to enjoy yourself. I'm mad because you lied to me."

"I only lied because I thought you wouldn't let me go."

"Don't worry, you're not in trouble. But from now on, I want full transparency, alright?"

"Alright."

"Now, go upstairs and get ready for bed, you've got therapy tomorrow."

I do as she says. I go into the bathroom. Brush my teeth, wash off my makeup, change clothes. I walk into my room and the rush that I had felt at the party disappears. I'm back to sadness. I press my ear against the closed bedroom door, and hear both mom and Annie snoring.

I take out my blade and start cutting once again. When I'm satisfied, I put it back in the drawer. Fuck! I was almost a week clean. I ruined it. I'm suddenly overwhelmed by anger. Why the fuck would I do that?

I start crying in frustration, and throw myself on my bed. Eventually, I cry myself to sleep.

I wake up to twelve missed calls from Eliza. What could be so important that she had to call twelve times? I open my messages. Eliza has sent me a link.

Underneath the link there's a message that says: "Wake the fuck up and look at this!". That's pretty strong language for Eliza. Curious, I click on the link. It takes me to a social media page - Anonymous_storksville. Storksville is the name of our town. I scroll down to the posts. My heart skips a beat. There are two posts. One about me, and one about Theo. Scared to look at mine, I view Theo's first. It's a reel. The video shows him crying.

"What's wrong?" says the voice of the person recording.

"I'm a man", Theo sobs. "I'm a man, trapped in a woman's body."

"What?!"

"Even after surgery and testosterone, I still feel like I look like a girl."

Some boys are laughing in the background.

"He's so weird and high", someone says.

"Don't you get it? He's a tranny!"

Loud laughter again.

The reel ends. I obviously failed to protect Theo. By the time he got to me, everything was already destroyed. Theo exposed himself while he was high. Something makes me click on the comments. I gasp. Hundreds of transphobic comments from the people living in Storksville. There are only one or two comments defending Theo. I can't believe it!

Suddenly, realisation hits hard. They've also posted a reel of me. I take a deep breath. Surely, it can't be that bad. I scroll down and look at the reel. It's someone filming randomly at the party. Suddenly there's a loud, very familiar sound. It's Elijah, slapping me. The camera redirects to mine and Elijah's interaction. I watch it from a spectator's view - how I throw the drink in his face, kick his crotch and flip off his friends.

Suddenly, there's a knock on my bedroom door.

"Alyssa, wake up. Mom made pancakes!" Annie cheerfully squeaks.

"Just a second."

Annie goes back downstairs. I bookmark the reels. Anonymous_storksville. I wonder who is controlling the account. It can't be Elijah, since he was sort of exposed on the account as well. I go downstairs. Breakfast is just as usual. When I leave the table, I notice more calls and texts from Eliza. I call her back.

"Hello!? Where the fuck have you been? Doesn't this bother you at all?"

"I'm sorry. It does bother me. The comments under Theo's video are crazy."

"What? No, that's not what I mean. I mean the comments under your video, stupid!"

My video? I haven't even looked at those comments yet.

"What do they say?"

"That you're a literal legend!"

Okay, now I'm confused.

"You're lying!"

"No, check for yourself."

"Alright, I'll call you back."

I hang up on Eliza and open social media again. Holy shit, Eliza was right. There are comments from Elijah's ex's saying that what I did was something that should have been done a long time ago. Comments saying that Elijah is a self-centred asshole who finally got what he deserved. Comments saying that I am a literal legend, just like Eliza said! What is this? The rise of Alyssa Tucker? I smirk. No way!! That smirk quickly wipes off my face. This might be the rise of Alyssa, but it's also the fall of Theodore. I put my phone down. I really hope that Theo is alright. I hope he hasn't seen it. He's my friend, and I care about him. About his well-being. I pick my phone back up to call Eliza back.

"I told you so!" Eliza says.

"Yeah, it's pretty cool, but did you see the video of Theo?"

Eliza gets quiet for a bit.

"I mean yeah I did, it's quite shocking. I don't really know how to react."

"Well, I'm fucking pissed."

"Yeah, I can't believe Theo would even get high in the first place."

"I agree, it's quite strange. I wonder who's controlling this account."

Eliza makes a loud thinking noise. Humming, followed with a gasp.

"Elijah!" She exclaims.

I sigh.

"It can't be Elijah. He was also put on the account."

Eliza hums some more.

"That's true, but who else do we know who could be controlling it?"

I look out the window. I look at Storksville.

"It might be someone we don't know."

"What are you saying? Both you and Theo were put on the account. It's obviously someone we know."

"There are so many teenagers and young adults living in Storksville, and it seems that a lot of them actually are this cruel."

Eliza pauses again.

"So you mean that it must be a coincidence that both you and Theo were put on that account?"

"Yes! It's not like I know that many people anyway."

Eliza gasps again.

"Yuki!"

"What? No, it can't be Yuki, she's too nice!"

"True…"

"We might never find out, it's best if we just try to forget about it."

Eliza sighs.

"Alright, I just hope that I don't ever see myself on that account."

"Yeah, I hope so too."

A few hours go by, and I keep an eye on the account. No new posts. That's a relief. After a while I have to go to therapy. I debate on whether I should tell my therapist about Anonymous_storksville. I decide not to. Instead, we talk about self-harm and ways to cope. Like holding an ice cube or snapping my wrist with a hair tie. I know that it won't be the same, but maybe that's a good thing.

The rest of the day goes by. Still no new posts. That means that I can sleep well tonight.

The next day is Monday, and I'm off to school. I find Eliza in the morning, but Theo is nowhere to be found. I immediately start worrying. I take a deep breath. He's probably just sick. He'll be fine.

I go to school on Tuesday, still no Theo.

No Theo on Wednesday either. Now I can't suppress my anxiety any longer. Wednesdays are the days when we study together. For him not to show up for school is insane. I think of a plan. I'll go over to Theo's house and meet with him anyway. I say bye to Eliza before going to Theo's house. She doesn't really seem to be bothered with my plan, considering she's already walking home with another group of girls. Arriving at Theo's house, I walk up to the front door and ring the doorbell. Soon enough, he opens the door.

"Alyssa, why are you here?" He looks shocked.

"I came for our study session. Since you didn't text me, I thought it was still on."

I look into his eyes, they're red and puffy. It looks like he's been crying. His hair is messier than usual. He looks terrible.

"Is it Wednesday already?"

I nod. He clears his throat.

"Right, come inside."

I follow Theo inside and up the stairs. His baggy sweatpants and t-shirt are making his body look twice as big as it is. We sit down on the floor in his room, as usual.

"So, what are we working on?"

Theo forces a smile.

"Theo…"

"Yes?"

"I didn't come here to study."

Theo sighs, and his smile drops.

"I guess I kind of knew that, your backpack looks very empty."

"I came here to talk to you."

He looks embarrassed.

"Talk to me? There's nothing to talk about."

"I'm talking about the party."

"Yeah, okay. I know, I acted stupid at the party, so what? Can't everyone just forget about it?"

He sounds irritated. I put my hand on his arm.

"It's not your fault."

"Yeah, right! If it's not my fault, then who's fault is it?"

"You were stoned, who knows what they gave you. I came here because I'm worried about you. You love school. It's not like you to miss three days."

The irritated look on his face changes. He starts crying.

"I can't go to school", he sobs.

"Why not?"

"Because when I got high, I exposed myself. I told the guys about me being transgender and about my dysmorphia. Someone recorded it and put it on the internet. The comments... Pages of transphobic comments directed towards me! If I go to school people will say that shit right to my face."

He continues crying.

"Theo…"

He sobs more and more violently.

"If anyone dares to say anything to you, I'll cut them", I say.

Theo looks at me with a surprised look on his face, attempting to dry his tears.

"You really shouldn't joke about that."

"Who said I was joking? Look, I want you to go to school. It's your right. You can stay as close to me as you want, just please try!"

He sniffles.

"Alright, I'll try."

"Thank you."

I give him a hug. He's so brave. I stay over at his house for a while. Suddenly as we're talking, a worried look spreads across his face. He's looking down at his phone.

"Are you alright, Theo?"

"I think you should see this."

He hands me the phone. I gasp out loud, not quite believing what I'm seeing.

Chapter 17
Girls

I look at Theo's phone in disbelief. Another post with a picture of Eliza. I scroll down to the caption.

__Eliza Goldberg's sexuality.__ Eliza reveals her love for her own gender. During one of the many parties she's been to lately, she was talking to a fellow student at Black Rose about finding herself. She told the student that she now identifies as a lesbian (she also asked them to keep it a secret). Eliza let it be known that she currently has a crush on her childhood best friend, Alyssa Tucker. If Alyssa was to find out, that would be *very awkward. Make sure to follow for all the latest gossip!*

"Oh my god, Theo!"

"I'm sorry that you had to find out this way."

"I need to go."

I get up to leave.

"Wait, where are you going?"

I storm out of Theo's house and run. Run all the way to Eliza's house. I ring her doorbell and Eliza's dad opens the door. He has a bottle of beer in his hand. Who drinks beer on a Wednesday?

"Alyssa, haven't seen you in a while. Eliza is upstairs."

"Thank you."

I go upstairs to Eliza's room and knock on her door.

"Go away, dad!"

"It's me."

Eliza gasps, but not in her usual way. In a scared way. It sounds as if she's going to start crying.

"Come in."

Her voice is breaking as she says it. I go inside and find Eliza sitting in a corner. She's staring out into space, phone in hand.

"Why are you sitting here, Elz?"

"No reason."

"I saw the post."

That just slipped out. I really didn't want to tell her so upfront.

"I'm sorry", Eliza says silently.

Did she really just apologise? I kneel down beside her.

"Hey, don't feel bad."

She looks up at me and nods.

"Is it… true?" I ask hesitantly.

A teardrop falls from her eye.

"Y-Yes", she stutters.

Eliza buries her face in her hands. I don't know what to say so I just smile. She looks up and sees the stupid grin I'm wearing.

"What?" She says, confused looking.

"I love you, Eliza."

She stares at me with big eyes.

"Do you… lo-love me?"

"I do."

She wipes the tears off her face.

"I lo-love you too."

She leans close to me, and kisses me.

It's everything I hoped for. It's fireworks and happiness!

We pull away from each other and Eliza starts giggling. I smile. Her bubbly self is back.

"What do we do now?" I ask her.

"I say we become girlfriends."

Wow, straight to the point.

"That sounds good to me."

Eliza giggles again.

"I'm sorry, she says. I'm just so happy. We're girlfriends! Gosh, I could've never seen this actually happening."

"Me neither! This is great."

"Where do you want to go from here?"

What does she mean?

"Hm?"

"I mean, do you want to come out yet, or should we keep it a secret?"

I think for a bit.

"I don't want to hide my love for you, but I'm also not entirely sure about my sexuality yet."

"I get that."

"I want to tell our close ones, but I don't want to be fully out yet."

"That's okay!" Eliza says.

She grabs onto my arm.

"This is confusing to me too. All I really know is that I love girls, and most of all I love you, Ally."

"I love you too, Elz!"

Eliza leans in and kisses me again. Her kisses are soft, but not too soft. They're perfect.

"Hey… do you maybe want to watch a movie with me?" she asks.

I smile at her.

"Sure! how about a thriller?"

"You know me so well."

She kisses my cheek and takes my hand. We get on her bed and she turns on her tv. We watch the movie. Well, kind of. We mostly just kiss and cuddle. Ironic how the one-time Eliza gets to pick the movie, we don't even watch it. We only watch each other. Eliza's gorgeous blue eyes are staring directly into mine. I gently caress the outlines of her face and body. My heart is beating faster than ever. I've never felt like this about someone before. I never want to leave. Even though she's kissed me several times already, I can't bring myself to initiate a kiss with her. I hope she doesn't think that it's her fault. A knot forms in my stomach, and I switch focus from Eliza's eyes to her bedsheet. Eliza and I… is this really happening?

"Are you alright, Ally?" she asks me.

She says it in such a concerned voice.

"Yes, I'm fine. I just…"

I'm interrupted by the sound of my phone ringing. It's mom. I pick up.

"Hello? Mom?"

"Do you mind explaining to me why Theo was just here asking where you are? You're supposed to be studying with him!"

"Mom…"

"He told me that you stormed out of his house. Haven't I taught you any manners?"

"Something urgent came up, and I had to go to Eliza's."

"What could possibly be so urgent?

I look at Eliza. She looks back at me in confusion.

"I'm coming home right now, and I'll explain everything", I say.

My eyes don't leave Eliza. They don't ever want to leave Eliza.

"You better!"

Mom hangs up. Eliza and I look at each other in silence.

"I've got to go."

Eliza suddenly looks sad.

"No, please don't go."

I lie down beside her.

"Trust me, if I didn't have to I wouldn't."

"Where are you going, anyway?"

"Home. I'm going home to… to come out to my mother."

I can feel tears in my eyes. I'm really scared to come out, but it has to be done. Eliza smiles at me.

"You're the bravest person I know, Ally."

I can't say anything. I finally grab her face and kiss her.

"I'll see you at school tomorrow", I say.

"See you, girlfriend."

She winks at me.

"Yeah. Bye, girlfriend."

On the way home, I can't stop smiling. I have a girlfriend. And not just any girlfriend - I have Eliza!

Now I just need to tell my mom. I hope she'll be supportive.

Chapter 18

Coming out

I'm sitting in the living room with mom right in front of me. She's sent Annie to a friend's house again, so it's just her and I. She looks very strict and serious, it's kind of scary.

"Well?"

"I'm sorry, mom…"

"No, don't apologise to me, please. Apologise to Theo for storming out on him without a word of explanation. He was very worried about you, you know."

Does she even want me to explain? I feel a fit of rage coming on.

"Do you want to know what happened or not?"

"I do, but it seems like you have no interest in telling me."

God. Am I really about to do this? Am I really about to come out to my mom? I don't even know what my sexuality is! I cover my face with my hands.

"What now?" mom says in a harsh voice.

"I discovered something about myself."

"So?"

"I guess I discovered something about Eliza too."

"What on earth are you talking about?"

"Eliza got outed online. This stupid account spread out that Eliza is a lesbian and that she's in love with me! I had to go see her, because…"

I drop my hands and face mom.

"Because I love her too."

Mom looks at me in disbelief. She covers her mouth with her hand.

"Theo showed me the post and I just felt like I had to see her, right away. You know, find out if it was true."

"And was it?"

"It was. I told her that I feel the same way. I like girls, mom. I like Eliza."

I see tears shining in her eyes. Immediately, I regret my decision to tell her. I should've just lied.

Suddenly, mom starts smiling a little awkwardly.

"I'm so proud of you for sharing this with me."

She isn't mad? I smile back. The relief is almost overwhelming.

"So, you're not going to send me to pray-the-gay-away camp?"

Mom bursts into laughter over my joke. "Don't worry, I won't!"

She pulls me into a hug. We're both crying. We hug for a long time. After a few minutes, mom lets go. She sits down next to me on the couch.

"So, do you have any idea of what your sexuality is?" she asks me.

"I don't know. I don't think I've ever loved someone like I love Eliza. I definitely like girls, but I'm not sure if I like boys as well."

"You don't have to decide now. That's the beauty of finding out who you are - you have your whole life to do it. And it's never too late to discover something new about yourself."

She puts her arm around me, and I rest my head on her shoulder.

"You know, I dated a girl once", she suddenly tells me.

I look up at her in shock. My mom dated a girl?

"Wait, really?"

"Yeah, I still don't know what my sexuality is."

"There are so many of them. How are you ever supposed to figure out which one is yours?"

"You know, you don't have to decide at all. Just love whoever you want."

I think about Eliza.

"I will."

Eventually I go up to my room. I figure I should call Theo. I really do owe him an apology. I call him and he answers almost immediately.

"Hey, Theo. I just wanted to give you a call to apologise and explain what happened."

"I don't think you have to explain."

"Yes, I do. You see, when you showed me…"

"I got confused when you just ran away like that, so I went to your house to see if you were okay. When you weren't there, I realised you probably went to tell Eliza that you feel the same way."

Wait, how did he know that?

"How…"

"Looking back, you haven't exactly been candid about it. Neither has Eliza. I found it quite fascinating that you never called each other out on it. At first, I thought it was close friendship, but eventually I realised that you're in love with each other.

Theo sensed it all along? I have to get back on track.

"I'm sorry for storming out like that."

"It's fine. I'll forgive you, if you tell me how it went at Eliza's."

I start to smile. Just thinking about it makes my entire belly flutter with happiness.

"I told her that I saw the post, and that I feel the same way about her."

"And what did she say?"

"She kissed me. And now we're dating."

"Jesus Christ, Al, you've got a girlfriend! I'm so happy for you."

I giggle. I have a girlfriend. A gorgeous, caring girlfriend!

"I do! That reminds me, how's your love life these days?"

"Well, you know, I don't think I should have one. Like ever!"

"What do you mean?"

Theo takes a deep breath.

"Well, I did some research and I think I'm aromantic and asexual… Surprise!"

Oh.

"I support you."

"I support you too, Al. And Eliza."

Everything is suddenly good. I have a girlfriend, mom has my back, and Theo is just focused on friendship and his personal goals. I've also found ways to cope with self-harm. I think things are really starting to turn around for me. Things are really starting to turn around for ALL of us.

Next day is Thursday. I dress myself in a black skirt, a pink tank top and a white zip up hoodie. Always the long sleeves, to prevent anyone from seeing my scars. I put some makeup on and go down to breakfast.

"You're in a good mood today", mom says. "Does it have anything to do with your girlfriend?"

"Alyssa has a GIRLFRIEND?" Annie says, big-eyed. "I didn't know girls could have girlfriends."

"Well, if the person you love is a girl, there's nothing wrong with that."

"Awesome! When can I meet her?"

I grin.

"You have met her. Lots of times."

Annie looks at me in confusion. Mom also looks at me, grinning as well.

"It seems that Annie has forgotten. Why don't you invite your girlfriend over for dinner tonight?"

"Okay, I'll see if she wants to come."

The thought of having Eliza over for dinner makes me weirdly nervous. She usually comes over for dinner now and then, but now that she's my girlfriend, it feels different. I don't hate it, it feels nice that we're dating. I'm not sure why I'm nervous at all.

"I can't wait to see her!" Annie cheers.

The doorbell rings.

"I'll get it", I say.

It's Theo. He's standing there in his usual jorts and a t-shirt, holding his school bag.

"Theo, what are you doing here?"

"I'm scared to go to school alone."

I sigh. "Mom, I'm leaving now!"

"Already? You haven't even had breakfast yet! Don't you want a ride?"

"It's fine, I'll just walk and grab something in the cafeteria."

"Alright, bye then. I love you!"

"Love you too."

Theo and I start walking.

"Is this weird to you?" he asks me.

"Walking to school with you? Of course not."

"I meant us still being friends, even though I'm your ex and you've got a girlfriend now."

"Of course not", I say again. "Eliza knows that we're just friends, and also, you just told me you're aromantic."

"That's true."

We reach the school, and we're really early. Theo still looks hesitant. I feel worried about him.

"Come on", I say with my most gentle voice. "It'll be fine."

With that, Theo and I walk into the school. There's not that many people but the ones that are there are whispering and gossiping as we pass by. I can see that it's making Theo uncomfortable. I glare at each and every one of them as we pass. They're all transphobic assholes, and have no right to gossip about my friend! We finally reach Theo's locker.

"Thank you", he says.

"You're very welcome."

"I don't know if I can survive the whole day. It feels like I'm back in Sweden."

I think about what happened to Theo in his home country. It hurts me. He's had it really rough.

"Of course you'll survive."

I put my hand on his shoulder.

"You're so strong, Theo. And you've got me right beside you all day."

He smiles genuinely. Suddenly, I feel someone pressing their body against mine from behind. They wrap their arms around my waist in a tight grip. One of their hands brushes lightly against my right breast. I recognise those hands.

"Hello to you too, Elz."

"Hey, Ally! Or should I say… girlfriend?"

She giggles. I turn around to hug her.

"Am I allowed to say that word here?" She whispers in my ear.

"Well, I don't hate that you say it, girlfriend."

She giggles again.

"Get a room, you two", Theo says.

Now we both giggle.

"Sorry", I say.

"How are you, Theo?" Eliza asks.

"So and so. I'm quite nervous to be back in school, given the recent chain of events."

"I see…"

The atmosphere gets awkward.

"I'm happy that we got the first class together," Eliza finally says. "We'll be right behind you, Theo."

We go get our things and get ready for class. As we're waiting for the teacher, some guy we're sharing class with suddenly taps Theo's shoulder.

"Hey, aren't you the tranny who got high?"

Theo quickly takes a step back, mumbling something inaudible with an uncomfortable look on his face.

"Hey! Don't you dare talk to Theo like that", I shout at the guy.

"Yeah! He's our friend, idiot", Eliza snaps.

The guy, who's name I can't remember, starts laughing.

"Come on, Goldberg, it's not like you're any better. You're a lesbian."

"You don't think I know that, loser? You think you have to tell me?"

"Your friend is no better either. Alyssa the harasser."

"I was defending myself", I tell him in a harsh tone.

The guy scoffs and pulls his fingers through his dark hair.

"I can't believe that Eliza could ever be in love with such an ugly, aggressive bitch."

Eliza turns pale and balls her hands into fists. She steps right in front of the guy and holds her fist up, right in front of his face.

"Don't you dare speak about Alyssa that way!" she yells.

He smirks back at her.

"What are you, her girlfriend, huh?"

He lets out a really mean laugh. Eliza drops her fist. She doesn't know what to say or do. I have to step in.

"She is", I calmly reply.

He stops laughing.

"What? So it's true, then?"

"Yes. Eliza is my girlfriend."

A disgusted look spreads across his face. An "ew" sound leaves his mouth.

"Girls should like boys, not other girls."

Now it's my turn to laugh.

"Not these girls", I say.

Eliza turns to me. She kisses me softly on the lips, then turns back to the guy. He looks like he's about to throw up.

"You're all a bunch of gay bitches", he yells at us. "I hope you all burn in hell!"

He runs off. Theo stares at us in aw. He doesn't look uncomfortable anymore.

"That was actually a lot less scary than I imagined", he says.

I look at the boy who's running down the corridor to get away from the 'gay bitches' - us. "Yeah, let's hope that was the end of it."

It seems like it is. Throughout the day, no one goes up to us directly. People just talk, and stare. It's tolerable. Towards the end of the day, I gather all the courage I can find and ask Eliza to have dinner with me and my family. I ask during the first afternoon class.

"Hey, Elz?"

"Yeah?"

"Are you doing anything tonight?"

Eliza's eyes widen and she looks excited.

"No, why do you ask?"

Her smile widens as well.

"I was wondering if you'd like to come over for dinner tonight", I say. "You know, your first dinner as my girlfriend."

"Yes, yes, yes!" she squeals.

The whole class suddenly turn towards us.

"Alyssa, Eliza, please be quiet."

"Sorry", we say simultaneously.

Eliza gives me an embarrassed look. I smile at her. She's so cute. I really am SO in love with her.

Chapter 19

Unsupportive

"We're home!" I shout.

Mine and Eliza's gym class got cancelled, so we walked to my place. Annie comes running into the hallway from the living room.

"Is she here? Is your girlfriend here?" She squeals.

She stops once she sees Eliza and I.

"Where's your girlfriend?" She asks in confusion.

"Right here!"

I put my arm around Eliza's waist. She giggles. Annie gasps in disbelief.

"Do you mean that… ELIZA is your girlfriend?"

"Yes", Eliza replies. "Ally and I are in love."

Annie's eyes widen.

"Oh my GOD! When are you guys getting married? I want Eliza to be in the family right now!"

Eliza giggles. She goes up to Annie and kneels down in front of her.

"I'm already in the family, ring or not", she says softly.

Annie tries to hug Eliza at the same time as jumping up and down.

Mom turns up in the hallway. "Hey girls, I didn't expect you this early. I haven't even started dinner yet."

"Our gym class got cancelled so we thought we'd come earlier."

"Alright. Well, go upstairs and I'll call you when dinner is ready"

"Sure."

We go upstairs and Annie runs back into the living room to finish her Barbie movie. We sit down on my bed.

"Have you told your parents yet?" I ask her.

"No. My mom is never home, and…"

Eliza looks down at the floor. The smile that was previously on her face is gone.

"My dad would beat the shit out of me", she mumbles.

My heart skips a beat. Does Eliza's dad hit her? He can't, I probably just heard it wrong. We've known each other for ages, I would have noticed.

"What did you just say?"

"Nothing!"

Eliza looks at me, smiling again as usual. So, I must have misunderstood her then…?

"If you say so."

We keep on talking. About school, about life, but most of all about summer. We graduate from secondary school very soon. We plan on going to the same college, but we also really want to hang out as much as possible during the summer. We keep talking until dinner is ready.

"Look, Eliza! Mom made pasta Bolognese!" Annie says, excited.

"Alyssa's favourite", Eliza says.

She's right. After all these years, she still remembers my favourite dish from when we were kids. We sit down at the table.

"So, how did you two know that it was true love?" Annie suddenly asks. She giggles as she says it.

"Well, I guess you know when you know, there's no way of knowing", I reply.

"Ally is right", Eliza agrees.

Annie looks disappointed.

"But how will I know when I find true love, then?"

"Don't worry, Annie", Eliza says softly. "You will also know, when you know."

Annie smiles at her. Mom finishes setting the table, and we start digging in. The food is good. It's just like Eliza said, she's already in the family, ring or not. We're all telling jokes and laughing. It's great. It really does feel like Eliza IS a part of our family. I find myself smiling a lot. I can't remember the last time I smiled this much. I feel like nothing can go wrong. I feel like Eliza and I will be together forever, and then die in each other's arms. After dinner, Eliza has to go home. I kiss her at the door and say goodbye. My cheeks get hot.

"I guess I'll see you tomorrow, I wish I didn't have to leave, though," Eliza gently says.

"Same. I just want you to stay forever."

Eliza giggles, as usual. I'll never get tired of hearing that cute, happy sound.

"Are we still on for a sleepover tomorrow?" Eliza asks.

"Of course."

She blushes. "I can't wait."

Eliza kisses my cheek one last time before leaving. Then, I go upstairs to start my daily fifteen minutes of studying. After that, I just scroll social media for a while. It's kind of boring. None of my favourite creators have posted anything new and there are no new posts from Anonymous_storksville. I decide on going to bed instead.

In the morning, I wake up to Annie playing loud music in her room. It's still early. Why does she have to be such a morning person? I get up and start getting ready as usual. It's just a normal morning. Mom drops us off, and school seems normal too. I have this weird feeling though, that something is off.

I find Eliza by my locker. I walk up to hug her, when I notice that she's crying. I lower my arms and take a look at her. She's wearing a low cut shirt. There are bruises on her collarbone and chest. Did someone hurt her?

"Eliza. What's wrong, babe?"

She continues to cry. The corridor is empty. There's only me and Eliza. I gently caress her bruised skin.

"Did someone do this to you? Eliza, you have to tell me what happened."

Eliza tries to calm down.

"My dad saw the video, and he went crazy!" she sobs.

"What video?" I ask, confused.

Eliza just cries. I take out my phone and open social media. I search for Anonymous_storksville. There's a new reel. I click on it. At first there's just clips of me and Eliza kissing. My jaw drops. We're kissing at school, at my place, at her place. Someone clearly followed us and spied on us. Suddenly there's a cut to a clip of me, cutting myself! A knot forms in my stomach. Someone filmed through my bedroom window, so I assume they used a drone to do it. Then, cut to a clip of Eliza's father hitting her with a belt in the kitchen. My heart drops. I hadn't misheard her. In the clip her father is yelling at her while Eliza is begging him to stop. It's so disturbing that I want to throw up.

I read the caption.

"Exposing the girlfriends."

My eyes fill with tears. This can't be happening! How can someone be so cruel? So unsupportive? Now I'm crying too. I have to comfort Eliza, though.

"Hey… It's okay."

My voice is so shaky. Eliza looks at me. I start drying her tears and push her hair back.

"It's not okay", she says. "My dad found the post this morning. It was brand new, and he was pissed. He started hitting me worse than ever, I actually thought that he was going to kill me."

Eliza doesn't deserve this.

"I'm so sorry."

"It's not your fault. I just don't know what to do. I wish I could just disappear."

There's a look of sorrow in her eyes. I take her hand.

"Listen to me, we are going to get through this together. You and me forever. Even in dark times."

Eliza bursts into a tired laughter, still with the sad smile on her face.

"Even when battery is running low?"

"Especially then. Now, let's get out of here."

We kiss. Eliza closes the locker, and we start walking out of the school, hand in hand. She is the best person I've ever known. It's cliche, but it's true. I love her with all my heart and soul. Our future may be uncertain, but I'm going to make this the best time of our lives!

As we're walking down the street, I feel like we're leaving the rest of the world behind us for good.

Chapter 20

Battery is running low

A few years later

Here I am, backstage. The sound of the crowd chatting warms my heart, yet it also makes me really nervous. I haven't played this song since I was a teenager. This is crazy.

"Alright, Theodore, it's time."

It's the stage manager.

I take a deep breath and look down at the bracelet on my wrist. I flip over the infinity charm.

You'll always be our Ally.

To think that the actions of one jealous girl with an anonymous social media account, drove them away from all of us.

Yuki. I haven't seen her either for many years. But I'm certain it was her. And I'll never forgive her for what she did to me and my friends.

"You guys better be watching this", I mumble.

I walk out on stage. The crowd starts cheering for me. I go up to the microphone and wait for them to silence.

"Hello, everyone!"

They're cheering again, even louder.

"Listen, normally I would start by playing something to set the vibe a little bit. But tonight is going to be a bit different, okay?"

I look down at them. Some of the faces look confused.

"I'm going to play a new song. Well, new to you guys, anyway."

The band starts playing the intro, and the crowd goes wild. Seems like they love the sound, at least.

"Now, what can I tell you about this song? Well, I wrote it when I was a teenager, and I've only changed one thing about it since then. Well, I guess not changed, I added something to it."

The suspense is building up. The band is extending the intro so I can keep talking just a little bit longer.

"I added a verse to honour my two friends, who helped me create this song. Unfortunately, Alyssa and Eliza aren't with us anymore... at least not physically."

I start to tear up. Get a grip, man!

"I'm really sorry, I wasn't expecting to get so emotional. Anyway, the song is called Battery Is Running Low. Let's get right into it! One, two, three, four..."

The drums chime in. The cheering from the crowd almost drowns the music. I look at each and every one of the faces out there. Suddenly, I spot two girls in the front row. One with pretty, blue curls, and one with short, brown hair. I stare intensely at them, as I start singing. I can't believe that they came all the way from heaven to see me perform.

The verse pauses, and I mime a silent call to the girls, still staring at them.

"You guys should've stuck around".

They both look back at me and smile, with a mix of joy and sadness, maybe with a touch of regret. They're holding hands, like they always were.

"We know", Alyssa mimes back.